GREATER NEED BELOW

By

O'WENDELL SHAW

AMS PRESS

NEW YORK

GREATER NEED
BELOW

By

O'WENDELL SHAW

THE BI-MONTHLY NEGRO BOOK CLUB
Douglas Bldg., 927 Mt. Vernon Ave.,
Columbus, Ohio.

INDEXED IN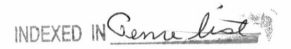

Library of Congress Cataloging in Publication Data

Shaw, O'Wendell.
    Greater need below.

    I. Title.
PZ3.S5364Gr5 [PS3537.H38745]   813'.5'2   73-144686
ISBN 0-404-00212-9

Reprinted from the edition of: 1936, Columbus
First AMS edition published in 1972
Manufactured in the United States of America

International Standard Book Number: 0-404-00212-9

AMS PRESS INC.
NEW YORK, N.Y. 10003

To The Memory Of
My Mother and Father

Who goes below to do a service rare,
For those who flounder in "The Monster's" lair,
And, at their source, encounter love, hate, even death;
Then flight from failure brewed within the depth,
To "Paradise," for just another breath.

AUTHOR'S FOREWORD

"GREATER NEED BELOW" is a novel based on some phases of life in a typical southern Negro-manned, state supported college.

Several years ago, I accepted a position on the faculty of a prominent southern college of the sort, and it was there, during a period of four years, that I gathered the material for my book; by way of observations of my own and those of others who related them to me as having been made at other similar institutions.

This book was not written in an effort to reform these schools of certain conditions as here depicted; rather, the aim is merely to present a few interesting scenes from the "inside" of a life which must needs be of vital interest to thousands of people.

—*O'Wendell Shaw.*

GREATER NEED BELOW

CHAPTER ONE

It was a summer, warm and languid, and Ellen Vance was spending it in the employ of Dean of Women, Marleigh, within the vine-covered walls of the Dean's cottage, across the street, not far off the campus of Northern University.

During the twenty years in which the elderly white lady had served Northern University as dean of women, she had contributed, considerably, to the means of education for several colored girls by permitting them to work for her during their spare time. Ellen was now completing her fifth and last summer in the service of the Dean whose interest in her was second only to that of the girl's widowed mother, Mrs. Annice Vance, affectionately called "Mom" by her two daughters.

The spring previous, Ellen had donned cap and gown and marched from the hallowed chapel of Northern University, carrying a parchment in her small hand, attesting to hard-earned degrees in education and music. When the ceremony was over, she had been gathered into the embrace of her loveable mother whose hands were gnarled from the too frequent manipulation of floor mops, needles and what-not, in a heroic and at last, successful struggle to see her eldest daughter educated.

This particular afternoon, Ellen solicited Dean Marleigh's advice, for now that the girl's education was completed, the matter of its employment was uppermost in her mind. Autumn was close at hand, and the sooner she could get commensurate employment, the sooner would she be able to lift Mom out of the scrub-bucket.

Too, there was Mae, Ellen's delicate younger sister. Mae had one more year in high school, but lacked clothes befitting a high school senior, and though she was marvelously considerate and uncomplaining, Ellen yearned to be able to properly clothe her.

The two women sat facing each other on the side porch.

"Of course, you wouldn't be able to get a teaching position in the schools here," Dean Marleigh advanced.

"But do you think the situation is fair to colored people who are prepared to teach? Thousands of colored people attend these schools, yet, there's not a single colored teacher in the whole system. Now, could you—could any fair-minded white person consider that fair?" A flow of maroon surged beneath the olive-brown of Ellen's smooth complexion, as her large, dark eyes met those of the white lady.

For several moments, Dean Marleigh was silent. Ellen's question had thrown her into a fidget, and a delicate pink warmed her white face, as her crochet needle slipped in and out of silken loops of thread. Frantically, her mind sought for an evasive answer. Finally she spoke:

"Well, you see," she began unsteadily, "the custom of employing only white teachers is something of a tradition in this state. The time isn't ripe for colored teachers here. Really, Ellen, you're not particularly needed. There's greater need below for you—" she nodded her silvery head southward, "below the Mason-Dixon Line. You're badly needed down there, Ellen. White people down there will not teach the thousands of colored boys and girls. Those thousands of eager minds need you and other young educated Negroes."

For an interval, Ellen was silent as the realization of the truth in Dean Marleigh's words dawned upon her.

"That's true, Dean Marleigh," she agreed finally, "and many colored teachers go to them each year; but I have my mother and sister to think of first. I'm told

that salaries in the South are extremely low, and I want
to see Mae through the university, keep up the taxes on
the home and take Mom out of the scrub-bucket. All
that will take a deal of money."

Dean Marleigh's crochet needle halted, and she raised
her eyes and looked at the girl intently.

"Perhaps, the question of salary shouldn't matter so
much," she said. "I should think you owe a greater
sacrifice to your race than to your relatives. My dear,
if I were young, colored and educated like you, I wouldn't
hesitate to go where I was needed most. Thirty years
ago, I left my mother and dedicated my life to school
work. Not because I had to, for my people were wealthy.
I did it because I felt that I owed such a sacrifice to
humanity. Why, I even sacrificed love and marriage for
my career. No people are in greater need of sacrifice
and service than are yours in the South. Really, I believe
you should go to them."

Ellen had been swinging slowly and thoughtfully. Sud-
dnly, she brought the swing to a halt, impelled by a conviction.

"I think you're right, Dean Marleigh," she said. "I
am needed in the South, and I—I shall go!" She arose
to her feet and looked out across Dean Marleigh' lawn,
toward the park-like campus of Northern University, as
though her eyes were seeing a thousand miles beyond its
ornate buildings, into the heart of the South which, during the moment, seemed to beckon to her.

Dean Marleigh nodded slowly. 'Yes, my dear," she
said, "I advise you to go. You're no doubt badly needed
down there." She arose and followed the girl to the
trellised gate. There they parted.

CHAPTER TWO

The days had sped onward, and it was now an early
morning of an early autumn. Sprightly, like the breeze

outside, Mom Vance went about her work of preparing breakfast, in the small kitchen of the home which she shared with her two devoted daughters. Mom was comely, brown and of middle age. Her lengthy hair was once black, but now its crimpy waves were profusely streaked with grey. Judging from the smooth contour of her once pretty, but now decidedly weary, face, one might suppose the grey in her hair to be premature.

Outside the tiny kitchen window, which shone like a jewel above the white enameled sink, the city was astir, beneath a chilly mist that hung from the sky like a damp, sagging cob-web.

Mom was disobeying indulgent orders that she had, the night before, meekly received from the two girls. The habit of early rising, to which years of outside toil had accustomed her, could not be shed easily in the matter of several days, even though Ellen's new position was to add a hundred dollars a month to the family purse. Once she had awakened, Mom's body and limbs actually refused the luxurious inactivity of lieing in bed, much as she would have at least feigned enjoyment of this latest formula dosed out to her by the girls.

The hour-old sun was piercing the chilly mist with pink darts when Mom gently tapped at the girls' door.

"Get up, darlings, and prepare for breakfast," she called to them.

"Mom!" Ellen compained, "you promised to rest these mornings. Now, here you're up, almost before sunrise. We intended to do the cooking."

"Now, sweethearts," Mom defended herself, "don't you worry about my getting rest. Since you've stopped me from working out, I'll have too much rest from now on. Just you young ladies hush and get ready for breakfast!" Mom's house slippers beat a tatoo on the floor as she hastened back to the kitchen.

Thoroughly refreshed from a night of peaceful rest, Mae bounded out of her twin bed and hastened to the bathroom. Ellen threw back the pale-blue cover which had encased her shapely body like a silken cocoon, and breathed deeply. She reached to the dresser and wrested from its embroidered surface a telegram which she had received several days before. She opened it, as she had done a dozen times before, and again read the words, "Avon State College for Negroes."

Avon! What a beautiful name for a school! she thought. Such a name somehow suggested to her, tradition, wonderful environment, and romance, perhaps. And just to think—a southern Negro college by that name! Of course, she thought, perhaps she need not waste any time in expecting to find a southern Negro school measuring up to the features suggested by the name. This would be contrary to the stories she had heard about such schools. At any rate, she enjoyed the wild imagination —the hopeful dream that the college would measure up to what its name suggested. As a matter of fact, she loved to dream; so much so that she was reluctant to permit this one to fade like the will-o-the-wisp at dawn. She yearned to live it; drain it of its fascination, to the last drop.

Whether or not Avon College should measure up to its very suggestive name, she felt that what she would be doing there would surely make it a paradise for her, and, in addition, she would be earning more money than she and Mom together had ever earned before. Too, Mom would not have to scrub floors any more, and Mae would have nicer things to wear. Of course, it all meant that she would have to be separated from them for months, but she told her-self that those months of absence from them would enhance the sweetness of the several weeks out of each summer that she would get to spend with them on vacation.

Ellen re-read the entire telegram, and to her, the words spoke volumes. It read:

"We accept you as head of Music Department at

twelve hundred a year.   Expect you here by September Fourteenth.

"Obadiah Johns, Principal,
Avon State College for Negroes."

She was folding the telegram as the bathroom door opened and Mae, refreshed and sparkling, tripped back into the room.

"Gracious, Ellen, don't you realize Mom's waiting?" Mae cried, as she stepped into a sheer pair of morning pajamas some kindly employer had given Mom for her.   "Oh, I see," she went on, "you've been reading the telegram again.   Gee! I just know you'll make good, dear!   Maybe you'll like it even better than you imagine."

"Mae, darling," Ellen said, "you're sweet to encourage me.   I know I'm going to like it all right, and I'll certainly do my best to make good."   She kissed her younger sister tenderly, then hurried past her to the bathroom.

Soon she joined Mae and Mom in the neat little breakfast room.   Three tempting discs of grape fruit were at as many places, on a spotless table cover, and Mom hummed a lilting tune as she retrieved a pan of crisp cereal from the oven and disconnected a bubbling percolater from an electric socket.

One again Ellen noted the three large aluminum kettles that sat on the back of the aged gas range—"Mom's experimental laboratory," she had often termed them teasingly.   Mom, stirring patiently with wooden spoons, and humming softly, had spent many hours of her spare time over them.   Strange potions of various kinds went into them and often came out in the forms of fragrant creams and pomades that Mom often emptied into the garbage with an impatient shrug of her shoulders, as if her idea of what toilet preparations should be was practically impossible of reaching.

This moment, as often before, Mom was lost to the

fact that the two girls stood at the table awaiting her, so absorbed was she in stirring the mixtures in the kettles. Ellen nudged Mae, and the two stood in silence, smiling impishly at their industrious mother. They would see just how soon she would return to earth again, from dreams, perhaps, of one day duplicating the success of that famous Madam C. J. Walker, colored, who earned a million dollars manufacturing toilet preparations.

Presently, Mom, suddenly recalling that the two girls awaited her, turned from her kettles. As quickly, Ellen and Mae looked at each other, then at her, and laughed.

"Mom, you old dear," Ellen said, "you're determined to get rich! All right, we shan't hinder you. We'll just—"

Mom, seizing the frying pan and shoving it on the stove, cut her short.

"Now you darlings just sit down and say grace," she directed as she deftly broke three eggs into the now sizzling pan.

"We prefer to wait for you, Mom. Don't we, Mae?" Ellen suggested.

"Certainly we do," Mae replied, then, "you'll say grace, Mom."

After several seconds, Mom turned the eggs into the tiny plates, took her seat at the table and reverently said grace.

"Mom, you're wonderful at fixing dainty meals!" Ellen declared, between sips of fruit juice. "I just know I'm going to miss your good cooking."

"Don't forget," Mom warned, "there're many other good cooks, honey. Why, I hear that the best of them are in the south. Perhaps you'll find one at Avon College, too."

Ellen sighed whimsically. "I hope so, anyway," she said. "Of course, I'll never find one whose cooking will please me as well as yours does, Mom. I just know I won't."

A piece of toast halted in mid-air, half-way to Mae's mouth.

"Ellen," she said, "I just imagine you're going to be so busy and interested in your work that you won't notice a difference in the cooking," then ironically, "perhaps, you'll even forget Mom and me, at times."

"Oh, Mae, please!" Ellen cried, shimmering tears filling her eyes. "Don't imagine I'll ever forget Mom and you! I—I couldn't forget my wonderful Mom and you, Mae!" The deluge of tears flowed down her cheeks. Her pent-up emotion seemed to swell and burst within her.

Tears streaming down her own cheeks, Mom was suddenly on her feet, hugging the sobbing girl to her bosom, while Mae, herself sobbing, kissed the two.

Like many other Negroes who had never been below the Mason-Dixon Line, they entertained exaggerated illusions as to the oppression colored people were forced to endure down there. Often, they had heard that in the South, Negroes were not allowed to walk on the sidewalks; Negro women were often the prey of low-bred white men; Negro men were lynched at the least provocation; Negro schools were deficient; ignorance among Negroes was rampant, and the first three of these evils were no respectors of place or person—down there.

So, to these three, it was sort of pathetic and ironical that Ellen must descend into that caldron of oppression to pursue her profession. Yet, it seemed to them noble and heroic that she was about to face it all so bravely. They believed that the South needed her.

Later in the day, Ellen's mind returned again to the telegram from Avon College, and certain tempting advantages again paraded themselves before her: A hundred dollars a month; experience; service—service she would delight in rendering to people who needed it so badly. Above all, Mom need not have to work any more; Mae could have prettier things of the sort so dear to the heart of a high school girl. Perhaps, some day Mom would be able to realize her dreams of getting into business with her toilet mixtures. Yes, Ellen was certain that she would find happiness in the South, despite its fearful reputation.

Before her lovely image in the mirror, after breakfast, Ellen encouraged herself audibly:

"Go!" she ordered, "certainly you'll make good—you must! You'll get accustomed to conditions—just like millions of other Negroes down there—and you'll enjoy serving!"

CHAPTER THREE

Dawn, swathed in a clinging robe of misty fog, had followed a clear, frosty night, and the morning of the twelfth of September held no promise of a rising sun. The entire city lolled beneath an atmosphere of smoke and dampness like a slumbering monster that had fallen in its tracks after a day of devastation. Already the inhabitants stirred about in the direction of factories and office buildings, and electric lights still twinkled through the windows of apartment buildings and flats.

A taxicab drew to a halt at the curb before the motly brick home of the Vances. The driver blew a husky horn and the porch light instantly shed a white gleam. Ellen walked out the front door, followed by Mom and Mae, the latter carrying her neat traveling bag. Goodbyes had been said within the house, and kisses, tears and admonitions had been profuse. Ellen stepped aside as the driver reached for her bag. She gripped Mom's hand.

"Be a good girl, darling," Mom admonished. "I'll be praying hard for your success."

"Thanks, Mom," Ellen answered. "I mean to do my best." She stepped away from her mother. " 'Bye 'bye!" she said just above a whisper. Then she descended the steps, in the adoring embrace of Mae, who escorted her all the way to the cab.

"So long, dear, and do be careful of the racial situation down there," Mae admonished, striving hard to suppress her tears.

"Of course I will, daring," Ellen comforted her. "And you study hard, and be nice to Mom. I know you will, though." Hurriedly she kissed her young sister, then, a lump swelling in her throat, she hastened to the cab and got in.

As the cab hurried off with her, she waved her handkerchief to the two. She was inwardly thankful to the driver for his haste, for now the tears coursed down her cheeks in glistening rivulets. For the first time in her life, she was leaving Mom and Mae. She was going to a very strange land—to her, something of an uncertain destiny—a place where Negroes were subjected, suppressed, lynched; yes, even burned at the stake! She wondered if she would have occasion to wish that she had never gone, that she had stayed with Mom and Mae, even though an only means of earning a living at home might lie in the operation of an elevator, or in the manipulation of mops and dust pans. She crowded the unpleasant thought out of her mind by considering the brighter side of the situation: She would actually be a faculty member of a college for her own people—at one hundred dollars a month! That would mean rest for Mom, and nice things for Mae! Certainly, she thought, going South would be worth it.

The south-bound train roared into the terminal, and an obliging porter escorted Ellen to a chair car. Mom had insisted upon a pullman reservation, but Ellen had declined it. The cost of this added comfort, she thought, fitted too well in Mom's purse—covered the cost of almost a week's ration of groceries for Mom and Mae. Then, she asked herself, why run the risk of being ousted from a pullman berth somewhere near or below the Mason-Dixon Line?

Ellen's only extra outlay for travel, beside a pillow, was a new novel with which she intended to dispel mo-

notony when her eyes should tire of the swiftly passing
landscape.

The chilly fog was general over the state, it seemed
to her, for, until a late hour of the morning, the train
thundered through towns from whose every building
twinkled rays of artificial light.   Happily, she contemplated the clear skies and glorious sunshine that she was to
find in the southland.   Finally, her eyes weary of the
swiftly undulating landscape outside the window, she
opened her book at the first chapter and began reading.
Save for casual glances that revealed that she was the
only colored person in the coach, she was soon oblivious
to all about her—lost in the story told in the book.

CHAPTER FOUR

A clear dawn followed Ellen's first night enroute
Southward, and the great city of St. Louis loomed in
the distance.   Her eyes felt heavy after a night of fitful
slumber, and she hurried to the lavatory and bathed her
smarting complexion in cold water, then followed this
with rejuvenating cream and a sparse coating of powder
and rouge.   She combed and brushed her dark, glossy
hair then returned to her seat.   Now refreshed, she recalled that in St. Louis she would begin the last lap of
her journey, and she hoped that from there, the train
would carry other Negro passengers.

In the great Union Station in St. Louis, she ate a
hearty breakfast of grapefruit, toast and coffee.   With
an hour to wait on her hands, she entertained herself
watching a stream of travelers as they trekked to and
from trains.   Happily, she noticed that a goodly propor-
tion of these travelers were Negroes.

Presently, the rattle of paper, and the restless whine
of a child, drew her attention to a dark-brown and buxom
colored woman at whose side were two brown children;
the smaller a girl, the larger a boy.   Sight of them

brought a sudden gasp to Ellen, for, out of a large paper bag, the shiny-faced woman drew a large, baked sweet potato and what appeared to be the shank of a boiled ham. After breaking the potato into three parts, the woman laid an end on her lap and passed the other two parts to the children. Then, pulling a small butcher knife out of the bag, she carved several hunks of the meat from the shank, passed them to the patiently waiting girl and boy, and mumbled some sort of thanks to an unseen provider. Sincerity shone on her countenance as she did so. Finally, she bade them eat, and beamed lovingly upon them as she joined them in ravenous mastication.

Somehow, Ellen's heart went out to the trio, in piteous sympathy. Never before had she witnessed such a scene. She recalled having heard of such, and at once wagered to herself that these unmindful actors in the eating scene were southerners; perhaps, of very humble station in life. The book she had been reading was some fantastic romance of southern Negro life, but its pages revealed no scene like the one she was now witnessing. The book was the story of a higher strata of Negro life, the like of which she did not believe existed in the South.

Momentarily she expected to see the woman withdraw bread of some kind from the bag, but none was made evident, yet the eating went on—each time, a bite of meat, followed by a bite of potato. She soon realized that the potato was being made to suffice for bread. She thought: No wonder that the children's stomachs protruded as they did! No wonder that the woman's face was so shiny and greasy! She shuddered as she wondered if such people as these, and such an act as they were shamelessly staging, were to have parts in the everyday environment into which she was going.

The chant of a fruit vendor tore her attention from the woman and children. She beckoned him to her, and, in exchange for several coins, wrested three oranges from his basket. She felt that she must give the little family

something. She went over to where they were and proffered them the fruit.

"An orange for each of you," she said to them, smiling
kindly. "Nice to eat with your breakfast," she added.

"Oh, yas'm. Thank you, Miss," the woman beamed
gratefully. "God bless yo,' honey!" she added. Turning to the little ones, she urged, "Say 'thank yo' ' to th'
kind lady. Aain't she purty lady?"

Obediently, their brown eyes sparkling, the children
mumbled thanks through filthy teeth.

"Where're you going?" Ellen question the woman.

The woman grinned broadly and anxiously.

"We's goin' to Chicago, Miss," she obliged, then,
"Yas'm, we been livin' out fum Waycross, Jawja. My
husban's been railroadin' an' he got us a pass, so we's
goin' to live in Chicago fum now on——" she sighed and
shook her head, "——I's mighty glad uv it, too, 'cause th'
po' white fo'ks is so bad 'round home. Don' you know,
dey lynched 'nother po' cullud man theah jist 'bout two
weeks gone——an' he ain't did nothin' to 'em, 'cep'm sassed
em a little 'bout short-changin' 'im fuh 'is work durin' de
yeah. I's powerful glad to be gittin' dese little children
'o mine up nawth wheah dey'll have a chance when dey
grows up."

Ellen was somewhat shaken by the woman's story, and,
for the moment, could say nothing; just stood looking at
her.

"Mighty sweet uv you, honey to buy fruit fuh us," the
woman went on gratefully, "an' we sho thanks yo.' Yo'
see, th' good Lawd——" But she got no further. The
train crier ended the conversation as he articulated Ellen's
train.

After bidding the lowly family goodbye, Ellen followed a red-cap to her train. After he had placed her
baggage about her, she dropped a coin into his hand, and
relaxed upon the spotless cover of a reclining chair——her
seat for the last lap of her journey into the heart of
the South. She immediately observed that the coach

was occupied by more than a score of white people, and
she was one of the only two colored persons among them.
The other person of color was a young man who sat several seats from her, down front.   Apparently, he was
absorbed in a magazine.   He was brown in color, and she
noticed his broad shoulders, and the dark, curly hair that
clung to his head.

So acute was her feeling of uneasiness, as she
approached the land of her destination, that she hoped
that the young man was himself bound for somewhere
below the line.   She noticed that the white occupants of
the coach regarded her more coldly than had those who
rode with her on the first lap of her journey.   Sharp, fur-
tive glances and flushed cheeks met her eyes when she
had occasion to raise them from her book.   She wondered if these smirkish glances were their expression of
resentment at the sight of a Negro girl reading a book.
At last, she concluded that she was surely having her
first encounter with Southerners, and that, perhaps, they
looked forward with relish to the attainment of the
Mason-Dixon Line, beyond which they would be spared
the ordeal of watching a studious Negro.   She noticed,
also, that she was not alone the recipient of stab-like
glances from the whites, for they were darting the same
kind of glances at the colored man down front.   She
wondered if he, too, were conscious of them.

Once more she returned her eyes to her book, only to
have them snatched from the reading by several drawling oaths that emanated, nasal-like, from the ,thin
purplish lips of a gaunt white man who stood, snarling
beast-like, over the colored man.   Immediately, she
sensed trouble as the reddened white man brandished
his fists at the colored man.   The former's voice rasped
loud in epithets above the roar of the train:

"God dam' impudent nigger!" he shot.   "Below the
Line, we hang smart niggers like you to tree limbs!"

"We'll settle it right here!" the intelligent looking
colored man countered, rising to his feet with clenched

fists. "Chicago University is my Alma Mater, and its pennant shall stay on my bag as long as I wish it to!" he shouted, then gestured as if to strike the hissing white man.

At this, Ellen got to her feet, unmindful of the danger that she might be inviting, and a few hurried steps landed her between the two angry men.

"Please don't!" she cried to the colored man. "Move back to my end of the coach, please!" Not waiting for his reply, she ushered him back to her seat, leaving the white man standing in the aisle.

Neither of the other white passengers interfered, before nor after Ellen had separated the men. Now, she and the colored man faced each other and he nervously shoved his hands into his pockets.

"Pardon my interference," she said softly, "but I think the risk you're about to take is unnecessary."

"I'm sorry, lady," he answered, regaining his composure. "I didn't know another colored person was in this coach. Certainly, I wouldn't do anything to endanger your life. You see, he took exception to the Chicago University pennant on my bag."

"Have you been studying there?" she asked, evading more from him about his brawl with the white man.

"Yes," he replied. "I graduated from there last spring. I'm on my way to teach at Avon College, if you've ever heard of that school."

Her heart missed a beat.

"I should say I have heard of Avon College!" she said, thrilled. "I'm on my way there to teach, also," she added.

"You don't say!" he smiled. "Why, this is indeed a pleasant coincidence! ah—oh, please pardon me, my name is Dewalt Brooks."

"Pleased to meet you, Mr. Brooks," she said, then added, "and I'm Ellen Vance."

"The pleasure's all mine, Miss Vance," he replied.

"May I ask where do you live, and what school did you attend?"

"I live in Halpern; fiinished at Northern University there last spring."

He smiled broadly. "This is wonderful!" he said, "that we'll both begin our first year in the teaching profession together. This your first time below the Line?" he asked.

She nodded with a smile, feeling a little nervous under his intent and admiring gaze.

He told her that he, too, had heard many unbelievable things about racial conditions in the South, and the altercation out of which she had just snatched him was, he supposed, a good indication of the condition they were being hurled into by the speeding train. He felt as if he wanted to be her protector as she talked on about her reasons for coming south: Because she wanted to give Mom a rest; she wanted Mae to have nicer things to wear; she cuold get no teaching position in her home city, and she understood that she was badly needed in the south.

"Our reasons for coming south are similar," he suggested. "We shall have much in common. I hope so, at least. We'll be among rank strangers—people of very different custom, I understand."

"And I'm so happy that you're along," she said, admiring him more every second.

* * *

Stealthily, the day slipped away as the thundering train dashed on southward. With the maroon of a setting sun came the train porter, who informed them that their next stop was also the place for their change to a coach for colored people only, farther down front, next to a baggage coach.

"Suppose we go through to that coach now," Dewalt suggested, preferring to thus evade any likelihood of further embarrassment upon reaching the next stop.

"I'd much rather," Ellen said.

The porter carrying Ellen's bag, led the way through the length of several coaches, to the one which was to be designated for colored people at the next stop. The first half of this coach was occupied by several white men who smoked leisurely. Once through the swinging door which separated this smoking compartment from the Negro section, Ellen gasped inaudibly, as for the first time in her life, she surveyed a "jim-crow" train compartment.

The compartment was hot and stuffy with the stagnant odor of smoke. At the lower end was a lavatory, minus a sign designating which sex it was for. The several seats on each side of this compartment were of faded red plush, and, reclining on one, down front, was the white news butcher, surrounded by his wares, consisting of magazines, confections and fruit. His cap was on his head at a rakish angle, and dense clouds of smoke curled from his pipe. He did not raise his head; just continued reading a pulp-paper magazine.

Ellen and Dewalt sat down in a seat midway of the compartment.

"We'll try to make the best of it here," Dewalt suggested.

"At least, we're away from your white adversary," she said, smiling.

"Yes," he agreed, his mind suddenly more absorbed in the fact that the train was slackening its speed for the next stop.

Presently the train was on its way again. Ellen sighed a little, and relaxed in the seat beside him.

"Well," he began, smilingly, "with this, I suppose we may as well begin to accustom ourselves to our new environment. Interesting though: 'jim-crow' conveyances, 'jim-crow' stores, 'jim-crow' districts, and 'jim-crow' everything else, I suppose." Irony was in his tone.

* * *

Night slipped over the landscape like a veil, as the train sped across the corner of a southern state. Their destination was in an adjoining state, and not until the following morning were they due to reach it.

Seeing that she had grown sleepy, Dewalt ordered two pillows from the porter. After at least an hour, the grinning porter returned with two soiled pillows, and an unconvincing apology for his tardiness. Ellen fingered in her purse for a coin.

"No!" Dewalt objected, restraining her hand. "You'll accept this pillow on me—please!"

Hesitantly, she yielded. "Thanks," she said.

After another night of fitful slumber, the two were awakened by the porter who informed them that their next stop was Avon.

Excusing herself, Ellen ventured to the lavatory, thankful for this opportunity to refresh herself before alighting at Avon. She gasped as she beheld its meager accommodations: Only a scarred mirror and a dingy commode, behind which was a pile of soiled toilet paper.

"Not even a wash basin!" she sighed to herself. She immediately backed out of the place and closed the door. Back in the aisle, she held her handkerchief under the spigot of the drinking water tank until it was thoroughly dampened, then re-entered the lavatory and wiped her face with the damp cloth. Hastily she ran a comb through her touseled hair, applied powder and rouge, then returned to her seat beside Dewalt.

Although he felt grimy and stiff, Dewalt decided to ignore the one lavatory.

"I hope you feel as well as you look," he said to her.

"Well, save for a slight headache, I feel all right," she replied.

"I'm sorry," he sympathized, then added disgustingly, "the whole thing's hell!"

The shrill whistle of the train pierced the early morning air, and the porter shuffled through yelling A-v-o-n! A-v-o-n! All right, folks, here you are!" he added.

Together, Ellen and Dewalt peered out the window at the myriad twinkling lights that greeted them from across three miles of rolling prairie, through the gray dawn. Avon College gave the appearance of a miniature city of lights, from this distance, topped by a brilliant and bigger light which was suspended above a pressure tank rising high in the center of the community of buildings.

The distant scene of flickering lights so engrossed the two that the train departed without their notice. The tiny station shed was dark and completely deserted. They preferred to remain outside on the gravel. From the station shed, a graveled road led, ribbon-like, over three miles of prairie to Avon College. No one was here at the station to greet them, and as far as they could see, no one was in sight.

"I wonder if we're expected to take the road and walk?" Ellen said hopelessly.

"Dam'!" he murmured to himself. "Surely not!" he said aloud to her.

Presently, the brilliant lights of a car pierced the early morning darkness, as the car ascended a rise in the road midway between them and the college campus.

Ellen's hope was lifted.

"Perhaps that's them coming for us," she said.

"Possibly so," he confirmed.

They stood amid their luggage until the car reached the graveled platform and stopped several paces from them. A young man, clad in khaki, alighted on the gravel, picked up their bags, and nodded his head sleepily, in the direction of the car, with an impatient, "To the college!"

Without further comment, Dewalt escorted Ellen into the back seat, then climbed in beside her, as the car sped out the ribbon of graveled road.

CHAPTER FIVE

Though a little jostled from the swift ride, Ellen and Dewalt, somewhat relieved of their grouch, relished the grandeur which confronted them as the slackening car approached the immediate campus of Avon College. The institution was made up of a community of red brick buildings, in the center of which stood a massive white stone building, upon a beautifully terraced knoll. They were amazed to find a southern Negro school so beautifully situated.

"Why, the place is beautiful!" Ellen commented breathessly, as they alighted before the large white building.

"A garden of Eden in comparison to what I expected," Dewalt said.

"It's a pity though, that the railroad isn't nearer" Ellen added.

"Yes'm 'tis," the khaki-clad student-driver interrupted, then continued, "but th' school's been out here over fifty years. Only college for Negroes supported by the State. I guess the white folks shoved us out here so's we'd be outa th' way."

"How far away is your nearest town?" Dewalt inquired of the driver.

"Our nearest town is Savant," the latter obliged, "an' we're fifty miles from the city of Braxton," he added as he beckoned them to follow him. "The Dean's office is down th' hall here in this building," he informed, "an' his Orderly'll assign y'all to your dormitories." After showing them into the outer office of the Dean of Men, the driver left them.

A few minutes later, they emerged from the Dean's office, following a student-orderly who carried their bags At a point on the campus, marked by a fountain, their ways diverged; hers leading to the women's side of the campus, and his to the men's side. The orderly beckoned to another khaki-clad young man, who came over and took charge of Dewalt's bag.

"Perhaps we'll meet again, later in the day," Ellen said with a smile.

"I certainly hope so," he replied. With this they departed, each lead by an orderly.

As they approached a new but sprawling dormitory, Ellen's orderly informed her that she was assigned to share a room and bath with another teacher. In her planning, Ellen had not taken this possibility into consideration, so, she was slightly flushed when the orderly introduced her to a Miss Madge Conley, her future roommate. The room was clean and neat, and Miss Conley was all smiles, as she went about helping Ellen to unpack her bag, and changing furniture about to make room for Ellen's small wardrobe trunk which was to follow later.

All this done, Ellen undressed and took a shower in the bathroom. Refreshed after the shower, she sat down before the dresser and massaged her face with a scented cleansing cream. Over her shoulder, she conversed with Miss Conley, whom she thought was quite pretty.

"How long have you been here, Miss Conley?" she asked.

"This is my second year," Miss Conley obliged, "and perhaps my last year. I'm dead sick of this slow place. So dam' many silly rules here, one's almost tempted—" Miss Conley stopped short, then, "oh, I forgot! You must pardon my swearing. If you don't swear already, you'll be doing it before you're here long. Why—oh, just call me Madge hereafter—that's my name. We're going to be good friends, I hope. May I call you by yours?"

"Of course you may. Ellen is my name. I just know we'll be good friends. Really, I think I'm going to like this place. It's beautiful!"

"It'll do," Madge agreed, doubtfully, then went on

with her aspersions, "but its management is rotten! 'Uncle Obe'—I refer to Principal John's—'Uncle Obe' is the nickname we've given him. He's no more than a figurehead here. The treasurer, Jesse Sales, is the real boss, and a hell of a dirty one! Stands in with the white people better than anyone else, so, 'Uncle Obe' and all the rest of us, have to look up to him. The dam'est bunch of Negroes in charge of things here that you've ever seen. I'm not trying to discourage you, dear, but—oh well, you'll find out everything before you're here long."

Ellen wondered if it could really be this bad.

"Well," she said with a sigh, "I'm here to do my best in the Music Department, and—"

"Yes," Madge cut her short, "I came here to do my best as the physical education teacher, but I found that one's best isn't appreciated here. They don't care whether they get your best or not, so, like all the rest of these faculty members, I do my darndest and collect my salary check each month, right on. These students—why, they do the same sort of thing—just do everything but study and yet they get by; so there you are: every dam' one of us wrong, from the principal down to the keeper of the pig-sty on the farm."

Ellen did not comment on the other's views. Instead, she sat down on the edge of her bed and cupped her chin in her hands. Madge said no more immediately; just went on pulling clothes out of her wardrobe trunk. Ellen was thankful for this, for she wished to think the situation over.

"There's a greater need for you, below the Mason-Dixon Line." Those words, in the voice of Dean of Women Marleigh of Northern University, rang in her ears again. She wondered if Madge, with her bitter aspersions, was a typical example of what became of young teachers when they ventured forth to the cause of "a greater need below." Ellen had been eager to devote the best in her to her work, but now she was given to understand that her best would not be appreciated. And above all, she wanted to be appreciated.

Madge jabbered forth again:

"Well, it's about time to get those gals out to the grid. for exercises," she said, as she stepped out of a pair of pink step-ins, revealing her shapely, pinkish-white body. "Dam' if I wouldn't rather be the military trainer for the boys than physical ed. teacher for these dam' old stiff-legged country gals! Not a decent figure among 'em! Every last one of 'em must have come right out of the wash tub!" Now, stepping into a pair of black knickers, she glanced over her shoulder and saw that Ellen was nodding sleepily. She came forward and nudged the sleeping girl:

"Honey, you're broken down," she sympathized with her. "You'd better crawl into the bed and get some much needed rest. Poor dear! I guess you haven't slept in the past two or three nights. Those hellish jim-crow cars!"

"You're right," Ellen agreed. "I'm practically dead! I'll get in bed this moment, thank you." She threw back the cover, crawled into its folds and turned her face to the wall.

Madge laced on a pair of white tennis shoes, over black-ribbed stockings, and hurried out to a large class of girls on the athletic field. She was a decided mulatto, unusually pretty, and the product of an Eastern college of physical education. Her feminine charms were tinged with a thin veneer of masculinity which, perhaps, was a hangover from the days of her childhood when she was often dubbed "tom boy" by her indulgent family and acquaintances. She was of a happy-go-lucky disposition, and, after graduating from college, came South to teach, against the will of her relatives who were quite well-to-do. She was free to spend her money as she pleased, and her lavish wardrobe attested to this fact.

CHAPTER SIX

Because of the rush of registration, and the general hub-bub of adjustment thereafter, Principal Obadiah Johns of Avon State College for Negroes, deferred the first faculty meeting until the first Monday evening in October.

A thousand students, and over a hundred faculty members, had dined upon supper when the campus bell, atop the half-century old administration building, pealed out a summons for faculty meeting. A balmy breeze stirred languidly across the campus, as lights in the various dormitories began to wink on, one by one.

Ellen put on a black, knitted ensemble, while Madge got into a skirt and middy.

"You look good in that," Madge complimented Ellen, "dam' if you don't! Its okay to doll up, since this is your first faculty meeting. Later, you'll get dog-tired of fixing up—just like me. I've reached the place where I don't even doll up on Sunday. What's the use, anyway? All the men have to sit on one side of the chapel, and the women sit on the other—the management's idea of discipline, you know."

"Is it actually against the rule for them to sit together?" Ellen asked in surprise.

"I don't know for sure," Madge shrugged. "I do know that the mingling of the sexes on the faculty is not encouraged a bit. Since it's taboo with the students, the faculty is expected to set the example. Just another of 'Uncle Obe's' silly inhibitions—dam' old ignoramus! He'll make you sick tonight, with his tirade of don't-do-this and don't-do-that. He'll give us a plenty tonight. Got to get his bluff in on you new faculty members."

Encouraging no more from Madge, Ellen moved over to the east window and looked out across the campus toward the rising harvest moon, which loomed on the dark blue horizon like a polished ball of copper. Distant

stars had begun to twinkle. It was a night of beauty—
one that suggested hushed romance. But for Madge,
with her almost insane pratings about the place, and the
poorly cooked food, Ellen felt that she could develop a
liking for this remote community of buildings. She
thought of Dewalt whom she had seen only twice since
their arrival. On these two occasions, their talk had
been only casual as to how they were liking the place.

She admired Dewalt, with his deliberate radicalism,
his frankness of expression. Tonight, in particular, she
experienced a strange desire for him. She yearned to be
at his side—to submerge her feeling of uneasiness in the
radiance of his strength.

Madge's monotonous voice again! "Come on, time
to go!" she said, then added, "what're you doing—
dreaming of romance under the moon? By God, you're
wasting time, if you are. Romance isn't tolerated here!"

With a start, Ellen recovered from her reverie and
followed the other out the door. The chapel occupied
the second floor of an old, brick building, the first floor
of which was the students' dining hall. Two entrances
led into the chapel; one at the head of a long flight of
stairs on one side of the building, and the other at the
head of an equally long flight of stairs on the opposite
side. One of these entrances was used by the men and
the other by the women.

When the two reached the top landing on the women's
side, Ellen caught sight of Dewalt as he reached the top
landing on the opposite side. Although he did not see
her, the sight of him eased her taut nerves. Later,
seated in the chapel, he espied the two young women and
smiled his recognition, receiving their smiles in return.

Principal Obadiah Johns sat on the rostrum, cere-
moniously regarding his faculty members as they filed in
and took their seats. He was tall, rawboned and brown
of skin. At least fifty years were upon him, or very close
at his heels. His feet were large and flat and, on them,
he wore a still larger pair of tan shoes. Across his long,

horse-like face rested a pair of horn-rimmed glasses. His head was long and bald on top, resembling the underside of an oval-shaped water melon. When outside, his headgear was a gray hat, several sizes too small. His suit was wrinkled, narrow-legged and of a faded blue color.

"Isn't he a hell of a looking something to be the head of a college?" Madge whispered to Ellen.

Ellen did not answer. She merely smiled, giving no hint of the disappointment and disgust that surged within her. Now, for the first time, she closely scrutinized Principal Johns. She had not before realized that he was so comical looking. The glow of the light against his bald pate made of him an animated caricature.

Presently, Principal Johns called the meeting to order with three loud raps against the table beside him. He arose to his feet, his eyes scanning his audience over the grotesque glasses. Then, gesturing awkwardly, he plunged into a lecture:

"Howdy-do, all of y'all," he bowed low. "Your Principal Johns is heah to meet you at Avon's first faculty meetin' for this term. For the benefit of new faculty members for this yeah, I'll say that just as sho' as fifty years ago a State Legislator lost a poker game an' had to take Avon College for Negroes in his district, as a penalty—'cordin' to hist'ry—you're sho' at a place where they ain't no playin' 'lowed—where evahbody's expected to work! Them that don't work ain't heah for long." He shifted his large feet and chuckled, then continued: "I say this to you new ones from big universities outa th' State: You just well make up yo' minds to 'bide by our rules, or else. Y'ought to know that that 'else' means— it means you'll be lookin' for a new job!

"Up in my office files," he went on boastfully, "I've got applications from teachers all ovah th' country, with all kinds of degrees; an' they're cryin' to work for any salary from fifty to a hundred a month. I won't discuss that point no further—a hint to the wise is sufficient—"

he chuckled again as his eyes fell upon one, a tall, light-brown skinned, sharp-eyed man of about forty years of age. He was Jesse Sales, the treasurer of the school.

"Mr. Sales," the Principal addressed the man, "stand up an' let 'em see you." As Sales arose to his feet and stood, Johns again addressed the audience:

"You know," he went on, a wide grin across his face, "that sayin' that money talks might be true, but this is one place where th' man that handles th' money does the most talk. That's Mr. Jesse Sales, our treasurer! He stands good with th' State Legislators an' th' white folks in general; so, you can judge 'bout how important he is. He's a very able man—been here, handlin' our finances for fifteen years. So, we all listens to Mr. Sales."

Sales was plainly embarrassed, but he smiled; a glint of pride shining in his narrow eyes. Bowing a little awkwardly, he sat down.

Principal Johns made no false statements in evaluating Jesse Sales' importance to Avon College, and with the State Legislators. Through those years, Sales' patronizing attitude toward the whites, and his tyranny toward the Negro constituency of the institution, placed him on a pedestal of authority above even the Principal. He was ever a willing tool of the whites, regardless of who suffered. Each year, during the hunting season, the sight of Sales tramping about the countryside with the whites, as lackey for them, was common. He was particularly adept at beating up unwary game for them, and often his buxom wife cooked the game they brought back. On such occasions, Sales and his wife took delight in beaming from behind white aprons while their white superiors sat around their table and ate the viands she prepared. Of course, they never dared sit down with the whites, nor in their presence, knowing that this would be taken as a gesture in the direction of social equality, a state of being denied Negroes by all whites in the South.

Obviously, Principal Johns' opening address, and his introduction of Sales, were his only object for calling the meeting. To Ellen, it all appeared useless and non-sensical—even comical. Throughout, she had clenched her teeth to suppress a smile inspired by the Principal's awkward contortions. Equally hard was her struggle to hide expressions of resentment at some of his implications and insinuations. When at last Principal Johns dismissed them, the campus bell was ringing the ten o'clock hour.

Again in their room, Madge predicted:

"He'll call a faculty meeting each month throughout the term, and you'll scarcely hear anything different from what you've heard tonight. 'Uncle Obe's' got no more business heading a college than I have to go out and take charge of the power plant!"

"His language is terrible, but I suppose he's more of an executive than a scholar," Ellen commented.

"Executive hell!" Madge exploded. "He's no more than a boot-licking figure-head around here, as I told you. That Sales Negro is the boss, and he leaves no stone unturned. He grins up to the whites and snarls down at the blacks. You'll get your first dose of Sales next payday. Gill, the 'cracker' general manager, is usually here with him on pay-day, and I mean dirty insults fly!"

Presently, someone knocked and Madge went to the door. It was the hefty dormitory matron.

"Well?" Madge, her eyes flashing expectantly, addressed the matron.

"Miss Conley," the matron began in an agitated tone, "the bell had actually quit ringing when you reached this building tonight. I was in hopes you wouldn't be coming in late this year. I reckon I ought to report you to Principal Johns right in the beginning. It's bad for you to be starting this new teacher out the same way. I guess —" She got no further. Madge cut her short:

"Will you please go to hell?" she hissed, then slammed the door in the matron's face and turned to Ellen with, "Let the dam' old mare finish her braying out there to herself! I hate her, and all these other Negroes here who happen to have a little authority! They spit on you then rub it in!"

"Why—why, you shut the door in her face," Ellen stammered.

"Yes!" Madge shot. "One has to take up for herself here! You have to be hardboiled just like they are!"

So acute was Ellen's amazement that she gave no further comment on the subject. When she had undressed and got into bed, she thought despairingly of what she had hoped to find at Avon, and realized that she had found just the opposite. Incidents here, up to this time, made clear an unuttered intimation that teachers, like students, could not be trusted upon their honor, by the powers that held forth. Why lock the female teachers in their dormitory? she wondered. Somehow, she wished that she could be as happy-go-lucky and fiery as Madge seeemed to be. She even wished that she could swear and rant like Madge, but her modesty was a barrier she could not scale.

She wondered what Mom and Mae would think, if she should assume a demeanor similar to that of Madge's; yet, Madge had declared that such an attitude was essential to one's well-being at Avon College. Ellen silently reflected that she had come to Avon with the determination to succeed, and if getting "hard-boiled" was the only assurance of success here, she must, somehow, get "hardboiled." Leaving these disturbing thoughts, she recalled that Principal Johns had announced that salary checks would be distributed from the Treasurer's office the following morning. Her anxiety heightened as she pictured herself buying a money order to send to Mom. She would enclose a long letter with it. She thought of how busy she would be the following day, and decided to get up now and write the letter to Mom.

She snapped on the light nearest her bed, and sat down at the library table and wrote the letter. As she sealed it, Madge, aroused from her slumber by the light, sat up in her bed, her eyes flashing in anger.

"What th' hell you doing with the light on?" Madge demanded. "Do you think this is an all-night joint where no one is supposed to sleep? Now, get to hell to bed and let a body sleep!" Following this outburst, Madge slid back under the cover with her face to the wall, thoroughly agitated.

"Oh, Madge, please pardon me!" Ellen begged, tears rising in her eyes. "I was just writing a letter home, because tomorrow—"

"God dam' the letter!" Madge flamed from beneath the cover. "Cut the mushy sentiment 'til tomorrow and give a dog-tired woman a chance!" she added vehemently.

Ellen said no more, but crawed back into her own bed, snapped out the light and cried softly to herself. How on earth could Madge speak to her like this? she wondered.

CHAPTER SEVEN

The following morning, the campus bell rang out the rising hour, clear and sharp, through the chilly wind which swept the foliaged campus of Avon College. Wheatly Hall, the two girl's abode, was astir with senior girls who hurried about, dressing for six o'clock breakfast. The titter of their voices mingled above the sound of running water in the general shower room.

From her bed across the room from Ellen's, Madge called to Ellen:

"Ellen!" she said, "you'd better get up, if you want breakfast. I'm not going. I'd rather sleep on, since I don't have a class 'til this afternoon." She frowned menacingly, then, "Oh, that awful noise out there! Wonder why'n hell they don't muzzle those catty—" she broke off short with a shrug of futility, then, "—by the way, Ellen, don't forget to go to the Treasurer's office for your check. I may not get mine 'til tomorrow," she added.

Ellen yawned and withdrew herself from the clinging folds of the cover.

"Thanks for reminding me, Madge," she said. "I've certainly got a plenty to do today."

She hurried to the bathroom and stood beneath a glistening spray of water, as she wondered what new experiences the day held for her. The shower refreshed her and filled her with zest. She dressed in fresh clean clothes, then hurried out to the cafeteria which served the faculty members.

Scarcely had she sat down at a vacant table when Dewalt Brooks came forward from somewhere behind her. He withdrew a chair across the table from her.

"Please pardon my interruption," he said, smilingly, "but surely breakfast will be more enjoyable to eat it with you."

"W-Welcome," she managed to stammer, between quickened heartbeats.

He sat down, his eyes feasting upon the reddish glow of her smooth, light-brown complexion.

"You're something of an elusive character hereabouts," he teased. "You'd better tell me how you're liking Avon by this time."

"Oh, I'm trying to like it fine," she replied, smiling, then added, "How're you liking Avon?"

He assumed a serious mien.

"Oh, I'm liking it all right, I suppose," he said. "Somewhat disappointed, though," he added.

"Disappointed already?" she asked encouragingly.

He nodded slowly. "You see," he said by way of explanation, "I've already discovered a lot of under-current stuff hereabouts. Had a run-in with the Treasurer yesterday, and he proceeded to try to impress me of the fact that he is the big boss around here. I—" he broke off at the sudden realization that they had not yet been served. He looked toward the steam table in the far end of the room. "I wonder what's ailing the waiters?" he said.

"Maybe they've forgotten us," she suggested.

"No, we don't forget in here!" It was the voice of the matron in charge of the cafeteria, which brought the two to attention.

She was now standing over them, fat, black and shiny of face.

"I guess y'all's forgot we ain't slaves in here," she said impudently, then added, "When you ain't here by six-thirty, your face'll have to wait 'til lunch time. That's what I say 'bout northern niggers: soon's they get to makin' 'nuff, down here, to buy a square meal, they wants to act big. Well, nobody here's gonna be bothered with 'em! They' all 'spects you to jump and run to 'em like they's white folks, but we don't do that in here." She turned and ambled away from them, laughing loudly and insultingly.

Neither of the two answered the woman. Ellen felt more like crying, so hurt was she at this sudden flare of sectional prejudice. Thoroughly angered, Dewalt bit his lip. Much as he felt like pouncing upon the insulting woman, he smothered the storm that raged within him. Silently, he escorted Ellen out of the place.

"Well, that's that, I suppose," he commented as they walked from the cafeteria.

"A decided cat!" Ellen said in disgust, then added, "but, I guess she's not to blame. She's the very embodiment of ignorance."

Presently, the two separated; she going in one direction to the conservatory, and he going in the opposite direction to his classroom. The campus bell was now ringing out the first class-hour of the day, and girls in dark skirts and white middies, and khaki-clad young men were hurrying to the various buildings for class-work.

* * *

Later that morning, Ellen hurried across the campus for her first salary check which she understood would be made out to her for a whole month's salary, dating from

the first of the previous month. She thought this very
generous of the State, for she had not yet worked an
entire month. She thought, a little nervously, of Madge's
prediction that on pay-day she would receive her "first
dose" of Jesse Sale's tyranny. This was the day to which
Madge had referred! She greeted a group of girls as
she passed them, and felt their appraising eyes following
her. She wondered, sensitively, what they were thinking
of her. Just like a group of students to become suddenly
silent and stare after a new teacher, she thought. She
hoped that they were favorably impressed with her
appearance.

Occupying the largest portion of the first floor of the
old administration building was the Treasurer's office
and student-depository. With a number of other faculty
members who murmured acknowledgement of her pleasant greeting, Ellen took her place in line before the
cashier's window.

Mrs. Burt, State home demonstration agent, entered
the hall and halted in line just behind Ellen. Mrs. Burt,
a light complected elderly woman, was known to "stand
well" with the white officials of the institution. Because
of this, her word went a long way at Avon College.

Over Ellen's shoulders, Mrs. Burt said to her:

"I understand that you're the new head of the music
department."

"Yes," Ellen admitted pleasantly.

"Well," said Mrs. Burt, "I'm Mrs. Burt. Principal
Johns has promised to let you and your male chorus go
with me to Braxton, a few weeks from now, to sing on
the program to be given by some of the State Legislators,
at the Gables Hotel there. I hope you'll have them
ready."

"I'll do my best to have them ready," Ellen promised.

"They'll want only spirituals for this occasion," Mrs.
Burt added, a note of warning in her tone.

By this time, the person ahead of Ellen had been
served by the cashier, and Ellen moved up to the win-

dow. The cashier, a young man whom she had not seen before, gave her an appraising glance.

"Name?" he asked.

"Miss Ellen Vance," she replied.

"Miss Ellen Vance," he repeated after her, as he fingered cards in a file. "I'm sorry, Miss Vance," he said finally, "but your check is marked 'hold.' You'll have to see Mr. Sales, the treasurer, before I can release it to you. His office is the next door down the hall." Ignoring her hesitancy, he looked past her and nodded his head, patronizingly, to Mrs. Burt.

Ellen stepped out of line and walked down the hall, the while wondering why her check was being held up. Perhaps, she thought, it was something in keeping with Madge's prediction.

As she tapped lightly at the Treasurer's door, she fortified herself with forced courage.

Presently, the door opened and Sales' secretary, a well-dressed heavily-built young man, invited her in. He directed her to a seat in his office.

"Mr. Sales is in conference just now," he told her, nodding his head toward a door marked "private." "He can see you in several minutes," he added obligingly.

"Thank you," Ellen said, relaxing in the chair.

Silently, as she sat there, she surveyed the room with its very modern equipment—more modern equipment than she had seen in any of the other offices on the campus, even the Principal's office. Sales' light-complected secretary sat at a large, green steel desk on which was a noiseless typewriter. At his side was a dictaphone, while behind him was a row of files that matched the desk.

Suddenly, a buzzer sounded somewhere about the muscular young man's desk, and, like a flash, he arose and hurried through the door marked "Private," closing it behind him. Then, coming through the open transom above the door, Ellen heard two men's voices that were strange to her. One was the unmistakable voice of a white man with a decided southern drawl; the other, she was certain, was the voice of Jesse Sales, and he was saying, agitatedly:

"Mr. Gill, this is the Ellen Vance payroll I was telling you 'bout. She's the new head of the music department, and she's waitin' on a hundred dollar check now. This job has always paid only ninety dollars a month 'til Johns got suddenly high-brow and sent North for a woman. You were away, so I held this payroll up. I don't approve of an advance in salary on this job!"

"Neither do I, by God!" Ellen heard Gill, the business manager of the institution, say. "Why'n th' hell didn't Johns get someone here in the State. I'm against sending North for these stuck-up—well, Goddam' if we'll pay 'er any hundred dollars! Let 'er in here, Lee!" he yelled to Sales' secretary, "we'll tell 'er what's what, and if the ninety won't do, she can get out, and quick!"

Ellen steeled herself as the secretary ushered her into the lavishly appointed private office of Jesse Sales, who sat at a large, steel double desk, across from the reddened white man.

Ignoring Ellen's greeting, Sales said to her:

"I understand you were ordered to come here at a hundred dollars a month—"

"Yes, I was," Ellen answered him.

"A mistake!" Sales said, shaking his head. "No such authority has gone from this office—"

"But, Principal Johns—" Ellen said "—Principal Johns telegraphed me that—"

"Johns telegraphed you a damned lie!" Gill interrupted her insultingly. "All advances in pay must be signed by me and Sales here. We ain't having no argument with you. Ninety dollar a month is what you'll take, else—By God, you may as well begin packing!"

"You'll please pardon me," Ellen said, "but, I'm here upon the word of Mr. Johns that I was to receive a hundred dollars a month. Of course, I had no idea that his word isn't authority here." She turned from them. "I suppose I'd better see him—" she added.

Sales shook his head restrainingly:

"I don't guess it'll help you any to see him," he said, then added, "We intend to tell him just what we're tellin' you! Ninety dollars a month is all you'll get, so it's up to you to decide. If you won't take that amount, you might go and tell him goodbye," Grinning smirkishly, Sales reached to a file on his desk, withdrew a ninety dollar check and shoved it into her hand.

Check in her hand, and in utter dejection, Ellen half-staggered out of Sales' office, through his secretary's office, and out into the hall that now seemed endless. It seemed to her as if the lump in her throat would choke her.

She found the conservatory empty of anyone else, and she was thankful for this. She sat down at a piano, bent over it and sobbed quietly. At last, her crying done, she recalled the days that had passed, and those words of Dean of Women Marleigh at Northern University:

"There's a greater need below for you—below the Mason-Dixon Line."

Yes, she thought, certainly there was a great need here at Avon College— a need for tolerance and more consideration for the feelings of those who were really conscientious in their aims to serve. She had come here to serve her own people, least expecting to find prejudice among them, yet, less than an hour before, she had been face to face with the most venomous form of sectional prejudice. She now wondered if the scant friendliness heretofore shown her by some of the older teachers on the faculty was based upon prejudice, too. Then this cruel insult in Jesse Sales' office!—

Suddenly, she wished that, like Madge, she could brush such difficulties aside with an oath, and ignore them; but, somehow, she knew that she would never be able to take life so lightly as Madge seemed to take it.

CHAPTER EIGHT

Days seemed to pass swiftly at Avon College.

Today, Ellen and Mrs. Burt had rehearsed the male chorus in song after song; all of them spirituals and jubilees. Mrs. Burt's interest had been boresome to Ellen, and the latter dragged her weary body to her room where she found Madge stretched across her bed. Madge wore a filmy pair of pajamas and puffed on a cigarette, as she fairly devoured a love story magazine. She rolled over luxuriously and raised her eyes to Ellen.

"Hello," Madge said, then, complainingly, "that noise in the hall is terrible! Those frisky little—" she stopped short for the first time noticing Ellen's unusually tired expression. "—Oh, what's the matter, Ellen?" she asked.

Ellen sighed. "Nothing, I suppose," she said, "except that I'm awfully tired and—and discouraged." She sat down on her own bed.

Madge studied her for a moment, then shook her head.

"Ellen," she began, "you're a darn fool to work so hard for the little money you're getting. You're too dam' serious about these blasted country numb-skulls you're trying to teach around here! They're not worth it anyway? The salary check is all you should worry about; just like the rest of us." She crushed her cigarette in a tiny tray on a nearby chair, then smiled. "By the way, kid," she began again, "I think you're getting the hundred 'bucks' each month hereafter. I went directly to Gill and got after him about it, and he said he'd see that you get it from now on." Nonchalantly, she opened the magazine and dropped her gaze into it again.

"Madge!" Ellen cried, "you—you got after Gill about it?"

Madge nodded. "Yes," she said, her eyes leaving the magazine, "Why?" she wanted to know.

"Well," the other hedged, "I—I didn't know you knew him that well—his being white, and—well—" She stopped short.

"What's his being white to do with it?" Madge's eyes were suddenly aflame. "He's a dam' sight more reasonable than Sales is," she added, then, "Now, old dear, don't get the wrong idea. See, he's particularly interested in physical education, and often he stops by on the grid and talks with me while the girls go through their exercises. I've got after him about Sales' dirty tricks before, and he's always had them rectified. Of course—" she smiled impishly "—it requires a little technique of a sort; that is, I meet him with a word to the contrary, a cute little pucker of the mouth, a wink of the eye, and he's ready to do anything for me. You see, I'm pretty well acquainted with men. They're all the same under the skin. They dearly love flattery, and your friend, Madge, can certainly smear that on them." With a boastful snigger, she returned to her magazine.

Ellen was astonished. "But, Madge, maybe I don't understand," she said pleadingly. "I mean that—well, you don't seem to realize that things are different here in the South. Frankly, I don't think a white man of the type of Gill could mean a colored girl any good. I wouldn't wish you to obligate yourself to him for me."

"Darn it all! you're being a little presumptious," Madge fumed. "A man's a man, black or white, North or South; and he'll go no further than a woman'll allow him to go. I know just when and how to stop 'em, and never fail to!"

"Oh, Madge—but—" Ellen was at a loss for words.

"Ah, 'but' your dam' silly brains out!" the other hissed. "Cut the sermon anyway and let's hit the hay! I can take care of myself and do a lot toward helping you take care of yours. Just forget Gill and me, and think of the ten 'bucks' they're going to add to your salary!" With this, Madge threw her magazine to the floor, got under the cover and turned her face to the wall.

After a shower and a massage, Ellen hurried to bed herself, but she did not go to sleep immediately. She lay awake for hours, thinking of Madge. She was fond of Madge, extremely fond of her, but Madge was so godlessly daring and outspoken! Somehow, she knew that Madge was extremely fond of herself too, , Often Madge's brutal way of reasoning cut deeply, but some sisterly deed of that fiery girl's always followed and assuaged the hurt. These little deeds usually took the form of a sympathetic caress, or a neatly mended garment, or perhaps a hastily prepared pot of tea when Ellen came in late, and any of a hundred such gratuities. Ellen realized that Madge was the type that cultivated few friends and appeared not to care that they were so few.

*   *   *

With the following morning came a cheery letter to Ellen from Mom. It said that Ellen's last money order had been received; monthly obligations had been met; Mae was still earning "A's" in school "and your Mom is still taking things easily, though my idleness often grows montonous. As to my stirring in the kettles on the stove: some day I may surprise you, my darling."

Indeed, Mom's happiness fairly radiated from the letter, and it made Ellen happy, too; so much so that the hours in the conservatory slipped by, that day, before she hardly realized it.

This evening, the meadow and clump of moss-laden evergreens fringing the campus beyond the music conservatory, beckoned to her more alluringly than ever before. Unable to resist them longer, she found herself going to them. The rare autumn breeze caressed her tenderly, as she hurried along through yellow, fallen maple leaves and withered vegetation on the ground. Farther ahead, Nature's autumnal carpet thickened, forming a golden mounting for the blue-emerald bosom of tiny lake Avon, as it was called. All this fascinated Ellen—drew her like a charm.

Soon, the cluster of buildings that adorned the immediate campus of Avon College, were at a considerable distance behind her, and she was standing above the tiny lake, gazing into its still water. She wished for Dewalt, that he might share with her the irresistible spell of this natural splendor. But how futile to wish thus, she thought. Rules!—rules at Avon College forbade lonely walks by unmarried couples.

She perched upon an old stump that reflected itself in the clear water of the lake, and breathed deeply of the fragrant air which rustled the evergreens a few paces beyond. She sat dreaming, only to be suddenly aroused by the crackle of the vegetation behind her. Turning about, her eyes met the smile of the elderly Mrs. Burt. Mrs. Burt wore a wide straw hat and carried a basket of wild greens, a late fall variety.

"Howdy, young woman," Mrs. Burt greeted her.

"Hello, Mrs. Burt," Ellen returned. "Gathering greens, are you?" She liked the idea immensely.

"Uh huh," Mrs. Burt replied, nodding her head. "Thought I could find another mess of them before the frost killed them. I suppose you're enjoying our lovely scenery," she added.

"Oh yes—yes, I love it!" Ellen said dreamily, then, "I intended to go on to that beautiful grove of evergreens over there, but the lake seemed to cast a spell over me."

"That's the old slave graveyard there," Mrs. Burt said, indicating the grove of moss-laden trees.

This information fascinated Ellen; thoroughly aroused her curiosity.

"Slave graveyard?" she said.

Mrs. Burt nodded. "Yes," she said, "slaves are buried there. This whole place—two thousand acres of it—used to be a slave plantation, many years ago. I don't suppose you've heard the story of this place. In late

years, they've quit the custom of acquainting newcomers
with its history. Thirty years ago, I finished in this
school. In those days, we took delight in telling of its
beginning and its history. Of course, things are different now days—" she sighed, a sigh that indicated her sudden nostalgia for by-gone days "—they seem to be
ashamed of its history," she added.

"I'd love to know its history," Ellen said, wide-eyed.
"Will you relate it to me?"

"Now, I surely will," Mrs. Burt promised, sitting
down beside the girl on the stump. "A good many years
ago—" she begain, "—shortly after freedom was declared, this State decided to establish a school for the
Negroes. They decided that only two districts in the
State were available for the establishment of such a
school. The ideas was to teach black boys and girls
the trades, and how to till the soil. Of course, the idea of
a school for Negroes was new at that time, and the two
white legislators whose districts they happened to be,
were each unwilling for its establishment in his district.
They engaged in hot debate. each offering reasons why it
should be established in the other's district. The story
goes that other legislators suggested that the two opposing men settle the question, once and for all time, in a
game of poker; the loser to take the school in his district
as a penalty. So, here we are. Evidently, the legislator
over this district lost the poker game." Mrs. Burt ended
with a chuckle.

"Quite interesting!" Ellen cried.

"Yes," Mrs. Burt went on, "the history of this college
is unusually interesting. Up until the Civil War, these
two thousand acres comprised the plantation of a rich
white planter who owned several thousand slaves; so
many, it is said, that he murdered them at the least provocation, and never missed them. He had their relatives
bury them in that graveyard over there. It seems a little
ironical that the old slaver, and all his family, are themselves buried on this campus—buried beneath an institu-

tion for the education of the descendants of some of the blacks whom he is said to have refused even the privilege of open religious practice, much less training of any sort. Baxter Hall, the big old frame building on the men's side, is, for some reason, named for him. He and his family occupied it, and it was called 'the big house' in those days. Of course, the Civil War left old man Baxter penniless. He didn't live long afterward. A few years later, his only son became a drunkard and lost this land to the State, for delinquent taxes."

The sun was a blazing ball, low upon the western horizon, when Ellen and Mrs. Burt started back to the immediate campus. Ellen felt as if she had lived through a dark, hopeless period in the forgotten past. The rising prairie wind beat uncannily through the parched vegetation at their feet, and, to her, its rustle might easily have been the ghostly trek of those slaves of yester-year, after a dawn to dusk of hard and prayerful work in the fields. Indeed, she thought, this was a different world to that from which she came—this campus of Avon College was truly a world of striking, blatant contrasts; some of stark irony, others of brutal paradox.

CHAPTER NINE

Next morning, during a class period, Ellen received a mimeographed notice signed by Principal Johns. It ordered all faculty members to meet in the chapel, with the student-body, at eleven o'clock. It informed that a party of whites, several of whom were State legislators, wished to inspect the entire personnel of the college. On the bottom of Ellen's notice, Principal Johns had scribbled a postscript. It read: "Call by my office immedately for instructions as to musical program you are to conduct for our visitors."

Ellen immediately dismissed the class and hurried out to the Principal's office. She knew just about what his

program would consist of—spirituals and jubilees!
White visitors to Avon College always demanded them.
Already, she told herself, she loathed spirituals and
jubilees.

She came to a sudden halt a few paces from the administration building, amazed at what she saw taking
place in front of it. A large bus had stopped before
the door and a group of white men and women milled
about it, talking and giggling boisterously. They made
up the legislative party that, each year, visited the school
unannounced. Ellen gasped at what she saw, for even
the white women smoked cigarettes, as if in mockery of
the signs that were posted about the campus warning
against smoking. How could this be, she wondered, when
there had been instances here of threats of dismissal of
even men on the faculty who had been caught smoking on
the campus. She decided, finally, that obviously, rules
for governing Negroes in the South—particularly at
Avon College—simply did not apply to white people.

She noted that Principal Johns was in the midst of
the party of whites, comically bouncing one of their
babies in the air to the tune of some ante-bellum Negro
ditty. She noted also that several male students stood
at some distance from the group, looking on in
silent contempt. The whites were plainly intoxicated and
careless of the flasks that were in evidence in the hip
pockets of several of the men among them.

"Well, where do we go from here, Johns?" Ellen
heard a burly, flabby-jowled white man rasp to the principal. Then he added, "We ain't got much time to
monkey about, if we're gonna see the whole circus."

Johns didn't have to answer, beyond a wide grin and
a nod of his bald head, for Treasurer Jesse Sales, the
gold teeth in his mouth glittering in a broad grin, stepped
forward from the outer edge of the crowd and directed
them to the chapel, himself hurrying ahead of them. The
Principal handed the white baby in his arms to a woman
in the crowd and bowed low, as she hurried from him

to catch up with the crowd now well on its way to the chapel.

"Make it snappy, Johns!" the flabby-jowled white man yelled back to the still grinning Negro, who bowed again and answered, "Yes suh! Got to run up to the office, then I'll be right on, suh!"

Ellen followed the Principal into the administration building, to his office.

"Here you are, Miss," he told her, handing her a paper on which the program had been scribbled. "You're to play for general singin' of spirituals and jubilees by the whole school," he added, "and you might play a selection on the piano yourself. Remember, what this school gets this year depends on the impression we make on these white folks, so, do your best!" With this, he hurried past Ellen and out the door.

Ellen followed him, her heart beating heavily in contemplation of what she knew she was to witness. Such humility, and such kowtowing! she thought, disgustedly.

"Negroes down here receive so little consideration," she told herself, "yet pay so much in self-respect for the little that they do receive,'

Somehow, as she walked along, she could sense the atmosphere of resentment which hovered over the campus as a result of the presence of the disrespectful whites.

At last in the chapel, she took her seat at the piano. Presently, the campus bell rang, and the students, many of whose expressions revealed keen resentment, filed in boys through one entrance and girls through the other. Down front, seated in a group to themselves, were the white people. One of them, a legislator, occupied the central seat on the rostrum, beside Principal Johns who stirred with feigned interest in his institution.

The women in the group of whites giggled audibly, and the remander of the audience was suddenly silent, as Principal Johns waved his hand awkwardly for order. Rising to his rough-shod feet, he launched into a blustry introductory speech.

"Faculty and students of Avon College for Negroes, hear ye!" he intoned, "This mornin' we're honored by the presence of Mr. Hicks, Mr. Riggs and Mr. Perry, our good State legislators, an' a number of other good white folks in their party. But for such good white folks as these, you boys an' girls wouldn't be here, an' you teachers would have no jobs! Praise be to our good white folks! Now, I want every grateful Negro—every Negro that's worth the salt in 'im, to join in th' song service an' sing such songs as only Negroes can sing! When th' singin' is ovah, good Mr. Perry, heah on the rostrum 'side me, will say a word to us." He turned and nodded his head to Ellen, then added, "Now, we'll sing 'Swing Low Sweet Chariot.'"

Weakly, Ellen struck the piano, scarcely conscious of the thousand young voices that rang out around her. Despite her overwhelming disgust, she knew that she must carry on.

With both hands gesturing in space, Johns beat spirited time to the music. He remained standing until he had steered the singers through a number of spirituals; one verse, two verses, and all the verses in each song! Finally, he nodded toward Ellen and announced, "Now, Ellen Vance, head of the music department, will render a piano solo!"

Ellen felt all eyes upon her, and her mind lurched about for something she could play from memory. At last, the lilting strains of a famous sonata trickled into her mind, and instantly the keys became animate at the skillful touch of her fingers. She whispered a prayer of relief when the selection was finished and the applause had died away.

"Now!" Johns shouted as he took the floor again, "we'll hear legislator Perry, one of the most noble white gentlemen in this State!" With this he sat down, a broad grin draping his long face.

Red and groggy from intoxication, Perry arose and strode to the front of the rostrum, and in a fashion typi-

cal of Southern whites when facing a Negro audience,
squared his stout body to a stance which bespoke much
vaunted superiority.

"I thank Johns for this opportunity to speak to you.
I enjoyed your singin.' It carried me back to my childhood when old Nancy, my black mammy, used to go 'bout
her washin' and' cookin,' singin' them ol' songs. This
State's invested more than a million dollars here to train
you folks, an' we're glad to see that our money ain't
raised you above singin' th' good ol' spirituals ol' Nancy
an' your other ancestors used to croon to white children!

"Johns here," he indicated the grinning Principal with
a nod of his head, "was chosen by this State to train you
here, an' he's makin' a darn' good job of it! You ought
t' obey 'im; I mean all of you—even you teachers who
got your trainin' up North in Yankee schools! Your
race needs more worthy leaders like Johns! He ain't
a uppity nig—ah, that is, he knows you and your
place, an' he knows the white people that's interested in
you—" Thus Perry stumbled on for over an hour, in
his drawling talk about "training the hands," a theme
long since made trite by the usage of Southern whites
when addressing Negro audiences.

At last, out of the stuffy chapel, into fresh air, Ellen
breathed deeply of relief. She hastened to overtake
Madge who had hurried out of the chapel and across
the campus with the bulk of the crowd. Presently, Ellen
was stopped by three whites; one a woman.

"So, you're the music teacher here, are you?" one
of the men demanded of her.

"Yes," Ellen answered him.

" 'Yes'?" he repeated, as if surprised, then, "where'd
you get your training?"

"At Northern University," Ellen obliged.

"Huh! we ain't a dam' bit surprised!" he spat venom-
ously, "for darkies trained down here wouldn't think
of insulting white people by tryin' to play a sonata!

Such as you ought to stay up north—you're bad medicine
for the niggers down here!"

Ellen's blood boiled at top-heat, but instead of giving
vent to the angry retort that surged within her, she
turned from the taunting trio of whites and hurried on
her way. She heard the woman of the insulting trio
laugh derisively. On her way, she passed other groups
of whites who strolled about the campus, accosting other
faculty members. Now, all of them flaunted their intoxication with reckless abandon. From each group of
whites she passed, she heard the words "nigger" and
"darky" muttered hatefully.

She felt desperately weak when, at last, she reached her
room. She found Madge there, changing her clothes.

Madge regarded her seriously.

"Did they insult you, too?" she wanted to know.

"I should say they did, Madge," Ellen answered
breathlessly.

"Goddam dirty 'crackers'!" Madge cried, then more
soberly, "I hoped that you wouldn't encounter them.
They stopped me, but what I said to 'em knocked 'em
cold. I told the 'peckerwoods' to go straight to hell!
'Uncle Obe' may hand me my walking-papers tomorrow,
but I don't give a cuss! Say, get up, Ellen!" Ellen had
dropped into a chair, so Madge tugged at her arm.
"Come on! I want you to point out the ones that insulted you! I'm a lousy pot-hound, if I don't make them
goddam rednecked bastards whip me all over this campus!" Madge's cheeks were crimson from anger, and her
dark eyes were aflame.

Ellen withdrew her arm, "No, Madge," she said,
"you shan't get into trouble!—you—well, you see, I came
here expecting something like this—only worse, so, I
suppose I can take it."

"But we have rights!" Madge cried, "and I don't mind
dying—"

"Yes—yes," Ellen cut her short, "we have rights, but
would a fight with that group of whites give us our rights?

There are other persons to be considered: all these students, your relatives, and—and Mom and Mae! Oh, Madge! yes, we must learn how to take things!"

Madge was seriously silent for a moment. Presently, she nodded slowly:

"I guess you're right," she said. Then she dropped the last garment from her body and hastened out of the room into the bathroom.

Ellen dropped limply across her bed. The sound of the running water in the bathroom lulled her into a deep, much needed sleep.

CHAPTER TEN

Late that night, the State Legislative party left Avon College. They left, not the place of serenity which they had found that morning, but one of riotous excitement and turmoil, for their insults had not been confined to members of the faculty. In their rovings about the campus that afternoon, they had also insulted many students.

Following their departure, more than a hundred male students took part in a parade of protest. They posted placards about the campus on which were scrawled the following protestations:

"Avon's Principal Is A 'Hat-in-Hand' Leader—
To Hell With Him!"

"We Resent Those Insults To Our Girls and Women!"

"The 'crackers' Smoked On Avon Campus—
Where was the Principal?"

"Damn Their Money, Without Their Respect!"

The parading students beat drums, tin pans, and whatever else they found that had the capacity for pro-

creating racket.   By order of the abashed Principal, the
campus bell was rung for order, but the mob of students
ignored it.   At intervals throughout the remainder of
the night, they kept up the din of racket.

The following morning, Avon College did not return
to normal activities; instead, the student-body and faculty
filed into the chapel at the summons of Principal Johns.

Ellen and Madge sat down in their seats, as Johns
rapped for order.   His haggard face betrayed a sleepless night.   Treasurer Sales sat beside him on the rostrum, silently chewing gum.   Presently, Johns arose unsteadily to his feet to begin a heated harangue.

"Students and faculty members of Avon College," he
said, his eyes blinking nervously through his grotesque
glasses, "never before has Avon College witnessed such
a demonstration of ingratitude as the one some of you
young men put on heah last night!   No mo' will such a
thing be tolerated!   Whoever said I'm a 'hat-in-hand'
leader is invited, by me, to come up heah on this rostrum
and repeat it; then whip me, for that's just whut you'll
have to do!   Now, I know them white people was pretty
rowdy, but Avon needs mo' buildin's, mo' equipment an'
things of every sort.   What them Legislators say to the
State Board of Education will determine whether or no'
we'll get the things we need.

"We're all Negroes, an' may as well make up our
minds to tolerate these white folks that can help us!   If
faculty members and students befo' us hadn't been tolerant, 'umble an' diplomatic, we wouldn't be enjoyin'
what we already have at Avon.   Now—ah—" his tone
became suddenly confidential "—we ain't wantin' our
good white folks to hear 'bout this demonstration, 'cause
they've promised to recommend a new dormitory heah.
You jest go back to yo' work an' study, an' forgit this!
But, I repeat my challenge: whoever called me a 'hat-in-
hand' leader—you's a lie! now, come up heah an' let's
fight it out!" With this, Johns waved his hand, signify-
ing that the meeting was over:

"Goodbye!" he added.

The students, thoroughly bluffed, filed out of the chapel in the usual order. Johns and Sales, grinning victoriously, followed them.

Ellen and Madge came out of the building close upon their heels.

"Good psychology, Principal," the two heard Sales say to Johns. They did not hear Johns acknowledge his compliment audibly, but saw him chuckle, low and heartily. Intimidation was an important part of his art, and once more, it had worked perfectly. Most of the teachers needed their jobs, and most of the students were there for the year, on one-way tickets.

"Well, the old boy's bluff went over big," Madge commented to Ellen when they reached their room.

Ellen nodded. "Yes, I see," she said, hoping that Madge would not go into one of her usual vitriolic tantrums.

"The dirty yellow livered coward!" Madge said, then, "You know, Ellen, I despise him!—I hate this place! But for you, Ellen, I'd leave, too. It's worse than the plantation it used to be. I wish you could afford to leave." Then more thoughtfully, "I just hate to leave you here!'

Ellen sighed. It would be terribly lonely, if Madge should leave, she thought.

"Madge," she said, "you're wonderful to think so much of me. Really, that would be more than I could ask of you. I'd be terribly lonely without you, but I wouldn't blame you for quitting after being here so long."

Madge drew on her cigarette and inhaled deeply.

"Well," she said thoughtfully, "I suppose I might as well hang on here, if I'm going to continue teaching. From what I can hear, practically all these Negro schools are alike—"

A knock came at the door, ending their conversation. Ellen opened it and faced Zelma Simpkins.

"Oh, it's you, Zelma," Ellen said to the dark complected, teen-age girl. "Come in."

"Yessum, it's me," Zelma said shyly, her wide, brown eyes shining in distress. Zelma was of poor, ignorant parentage, her father being a laborer about the power plant. She was an admirable student in the high school division, and assisted her mother with the washings they solicited from the faculty members. Out of pity, Ellen and Madge occasionally gave them delicate things to wash. They particularly admired this little girl who, most always, wore a broad, infectious smile. As a result of her perennial sunshine, their cast-off clothing always went to Zelma.

But, this morning, they missed Zelma's accustomed smile. The child, her lips acquiver, stood facing them and toying nervously, with a string of wooden beads about her throat.

"Well, what is it, Zelma?" Ellen asked sympathetically.

"We—we're havin' to move, Miss Ellen," Zelma said, bursting into tears.

Madge was next to speak: "Where to?" she asked.

Zelma got hold of herself and shook her head.

"I don't know yet." she said. "Dad—he ain't found no place yet, but we got to get off the campus. You see, Mr. Sales fired him yesterday evenin,' an' had our things set out this mornin.' "

"Fired him for what?" the question was for Zelma, but Madge's eyes met those of Ellen's, and the two awaited Zelma's reply.

"Well, Mr. Sales was mad at daddy because Mr. Gill raised his salary to fifty dollars a month. He said daddy wasn't worth it, an' said he was gonna fire 'im next time any empty oil drums was left about. Daddy was sick yesterday an' didn't get 'em all put away, so Mr. Sales come and told 'im to get off the campus as quick as possible. This mornin' some men come and set our things out."

This inflamed Ellen's already smouldering contempt for Jesse Sales.

"Your father was surely entitled to more time than that to get out!" she said to the girl.

"I should say as much!" Madge put in. "What's your mother doing, Zelma?" she asked.

"She's cryin' an' tryin' to finish packin' in the yard. Daddy's gone to Savant to try to find a house to move in."

The eyes of the two teachers met, as their minds sought for an idea.

Presently, Ellen exclaimed, "I have it! We'll appeal to Principal Johns! Surely he'll not tolerate such injustice as this."

Madge shrugged doubtfully.

"I'll bet you he will," she said. "Sales is the last word here. Sneaking rat!" she added disgustedly.

*   *   *

Principal Johns' secretary, a mannishly dressed, old-maidish woman of about forty, admitted them to his outer office. She gasped and gestured sympathetically when Ellen and Madge explained to her their mission. After satisfying herself that their mission was of sufficient importance for the Principal's attention, she entered a door marked "Private," and returned, presently, followed by Principal Johns. He was visibly irked and stared insolently at them over his grotesque glasses. That his secretary had explained the situation to him was evident in his tone.

"Young women, I'm awfully busy," he said. "I know all 'bout Mr. Sales an' Simpkins. I trust in Mr. Sales' judgment in the matter!"

Madge, of course, was the first of the two teachers to speak:

"But, couldn't he have given them more time to get out?" she asked.

"I've got no time for such trifles!" Johns snapped, his

hands awkwardly emphasizing his words. "Mr. Sales understands these common laborers," he added hotly, "an' knows just how to deal with 'em!" With this, he stepped back into his private office and closed the door in their faces.

Madge turned to Zelma. "This is outrageous!" she said. "Show us to your house. Maybe we can help your mother somehow."

The three hurried out of Principal Johns' office and across to the rear edge of the campus. They found that the unfortunate family had occupied a ramshackle house of three or four rooms—a house that was one of a slummy row of shacks that were inhabited by laborers in the employ of the institution.

Zelma's mother was on the porch of the shack, surrounded by several pieces of delapidated furniture, while her father was busy placing things into a mule-drawn wagon. Jesse Sales stood at a distance in the front yard, watching them.

Zelma hastened on to the house, leaving the two teachers behind her in the yard.

"This is a dirty deal for them!" Madge said to Ellen, knowing that Sales heard her.

At this, Sales came across the weed-grown yard to where they stood.

He said, apologetically: "It's disgusting that I always have to stand by and see that these laborers take no more than what belongs to 'em when I fire 'em!"

"I see little that they could take," Madge said contemptuously, then nodded toward the house, "That shack isn't fit to live in," she added.

Sales ignored her thrust.

"I'm taking no chances," he said. "I'm rushing this one off the State's property today."

"Well," Madge answered derisively, "you're dirty not to allow them time to find a place to go!"

Sales flushed suddenly. "My rule is to hustle 'em out

quick as possible! They can worry about where to go when they're off the State's property!"

Madge stared at him cuttingly, then turned from him and followed Ellen around the house. They found Mrs. Simpkins tenderly tucking a ragged quilt about an invalid boy, seven or eight years old. His withered legs dangled about a small cane-bottomed chair on which he sat, as Zelma and the mother lifted him about.

Ellen hurried to the mother's side.

"May we help you in any way?" she asked the dejected woman.

While she awaited the woman's answer, she felt a lump rising in her throat, and blinked her eyes to keep back the tears.

Mrs. Simpkins was haggard and frail. Worry over her helpless boy, and hard work, coupled with constant and bitter distrust of the strata of society that the two teachers represented, were revealed in the gleam of her eyes. Ellen's kind solicitation brought a faint smile to the woman's wrinkled face, and she said:

"Sweet uv you, honey, but I reckon not. I think me and Zelma can get our baby to the wagon all right. Thank you jest the same."

"How far will you have to go to a new home?" Madge asked the pitiful mother.

"Jest 'bout ten miles frum here, mam," she replied nervously.

"Well, it'll be tough on this child to ride that far in the wagon, I should think," Madge commented, glancing at Sales' car, parked outside the gate. "Wait a minute," she added, then turned from her and hurried around the house to where Sales stood.

To Sales, she said: "Would you have time to drive the little crippled boy about ten miles, to where they're moving?"

Sales shrugged disgustedly. "No!" he said dryly.

"Well, would you lend me your car long enough to drive him?" she countered.

Sales shrugged again, defiantly:

"I don't even permit my wife to drive my car!" he snapped.

"Your pretty heartless!" she told him bitterly.

He grinned mirthlessly. "It's all a cold business matter with me," he answered.

Madge could hold in no longer:

"I see," she said. "You have no feelings, you goddam dirty tyrant!" Her voice rang menacingly on these last words.

Abruptly, Sales turned from her, got into his car and drove off the premises.

He left Madge angrily exasperated. Before she moved to return to the house, she felt Ellen's hand on her arm.

"They're off all right, Madge," Ellen said. "We managed to pad the little boy with pillows," she explained.

Madge was flushed and hurt.

"This is plain tyranny!" she said, shaking her head. "Zelma and that poor little innocent cripple!" she added.

"Well," Ellen said a little breathlessly, "I suppose there's nothing more that we can do for them." She gripped the other's arm. "Come along, dear. We'd better get back to the campus and try to forget this whole thing."

Side by side, they walked back to the immediate campus, both conscious and resentful of the utter disregard for what was right, by the powers that be at Avon College.

CHAPTER ELEVEN

The golden autumn was nearly past, and the magic of its inevitable touch had tinged the level table of prairieland surrounding Avon College with the deep brown of fallen leaves and dead vegetation. Prolonged chill was the order of the season. Already, the ornate buildings and ribbons of pavement on the campus had flaunted more than one mantle of flakey frost. The days, with their grinding routine of eat, sleep and work, had long since grown monotonous to Ellen.

Came another "calling night" when the single men on the faculty were permitted to call on the single women. In the reception room of Wheatley Hall, Ellen and Dewalt sat side by side on a divan. Their conversation drifted from expressions of endearment for each other to an exchange of opinions about conditions at Avon College.

"These students need something more than just the books they study," Ellen commented thoughtfully. "They get almost no cultural training," she went on. "They're herded into their dining hall each meal time and fed in a manner hardly different from that of feeding animals. No emphasis on how to eat," she shrugged, "how to be well-mannered, or anything of the sort! And there's much that could be done for the families of those laborers living back of the campus. Oh, Dewalt," she went on whimsically, "I yearn to go among them and teach them cleanliness; the importance of keeping neat yards, cultivating flowers, and such things."

"But, just you try helping the living condition of those laborers!" Dewalt challenged.

"Of course, I know that attempting such a thing would mean social suicide around here," she said, "but perhaps I wouldn't care anyway. I am something of a social outcast here as it is. As a matter of fact, I've already tried to interest several other faculty members in such work, but they merely shrugged and laughed at me. I even suggested such a spare-time social program to the Principal, and he looked at me as if he thought I had lost my mind. When he was through gaping at me, he shook his head and said that it would be just like casting pearls before swine. Can you imagine such an opinion coming from the head of an educational institution?"

Dewalt had been quietly studying her with adoration in his eyes; deeply admiring her idealism. Somehow, he knew that this whimsy of hers was the expression of a pure and unselfish heart.

He nodded slowly and thoughtfully:

"Yes," he said, "when I think of the effect this so-called education seems to have on, perhaps, too many Negroes. It changes them, all right; turns them into egotistic fools. Think of it: the parents of most of us belonged to this laboring class, otherwise, many of us wouldn't have education in its various degrees. To my mind, education misses of its aim when it fails to endow one with the desire to reach down and help those below him. In too many instances, formal education seems to rob young Negroes of something. They come out of the schools with their degrees, and nothing else save an egotistic veneer. Just like that table there: scratch from it its veneered surface, and you have nothing left but the rough wood. Many of them leave the schools completely divested of initiative and originality, if they ever before had any. A ready-made job is what they are looking for when they come out. To them, all the problems confronting the race are solved once they get a job." He laughed mirthlessly, then went on: "But, you're an exception, Ellen. You've come here and found something beyond the immediate confines of your job that should be done, and you worry because you are not permitted to do it.

"As for me," he continued, "maybe I'm an exception, too. I'm not satisfied with the confinement of a mere job. I want to do something for the race on a broader scale. Negroes need something more fundamental and practical in the way of training. These young people are in need of a training of a sort that will stimulate the will and cultivate initiative. We must remember that the educational system in this country is designed primarily for whites, and it fits them for their problems. But it falls short, generally speaking, of fitting the Negro. I look forward to, some day, working out a university curriculum designed especially for what I think are the

needs of the Negro. Such a thing would be revolutionary, all right, but who can say that it would not be just
the thing that the race needs?"

When he had finished, Ellen was too enthralled to
speak. She was seeing such a revolutionary university,
with him as its head—all in her imagination.

Presently, she felt the warmth of his hand upon hers
and the vision of his dream-university vanished and she
was back to earth, facing reality—the reality of a desire
to be drawn close to him by his muscular arms and kissed
passionately. Somehow, she knew that from this
moment on, she belonged to him.

He felt the quickened beat of her pulse, and yearned
to gather her into his arms and plant burning kisses upon
her lips, her smooth brown throat and her dark, luxuriant
hair. But this was not the place, and he had to satisfy
himself with merely gripping her small hand tighter.

"Ellen," he said hoarsely, "there's a possibility of our
having to separate one of these days, but I will always
love you! Will you remember that?"

She was suddenly uneasy at his mention of separation,
and felt desperately in need of him.

"I can never forget it!" she whispered breathlessly,
shaking her head. Then, "But, Dewalt, why contem-
plate separation?" She looked him in the eyes intently,
pleadingly.

He stirred nervously.

"Because, I may have to leave this place any time,
Ellen," he said. "You see," he went on, "I can't seem
to adjust myself here. Consider my predicament: I
came here under the impression that I was to head a real
department of business administration—they called it
that—and what have I found?" he shrugged disgustedly.
"Only a stuffy room equipped with eight battered type-
writers and a few ragged elementary text-books. Yet, a
number of students will leave my department, next spring,
with the degree of B. S. in business administration. Think
of what a joke it will be—and I will be a party to it!

What will they be able to do besides running a typewriter and defining the law of supply and demand? What will they know about marketing—marketing even the products they have learned to produce here on the farm? What will they know about investments, advertising, salesmanship? Nothing!—absolutely nothing!

"You know," he went on, "these white officials, even the philanthropists who donate large sums of money to such schools as this, are strange benefactors, indeed. They give and appropriate millions to educate the Negro in the fine arts, such as music, yet, in comparison, they give almost nothing toward training Negroes in business and economics—the very things that are the backbone of this wealthiest of all countries. Sometimes when I hear them extolling Negroes for their so-called 'natural music and artistic talent,' I imagine that they're laughing to themselves at how easily they are able to thus steer us away from the ambition to master the very things that have made them the owners of the earth.

"But, coming back to the immediate question of the possibility of our separation:" he continued, "I never was adept at kowtowing, and that's just what one is expected to do here. We must kowtow to these executives while they spend most of their time kowtowing to the whites. I'm sick of it! My patience is strained, which means that the break is inevitable. When it comes, I know I'll have to leave!"

His lengthy explanation did nothing toward reconciling Ellen to the thought of having to give him up.

"I admit that the attitude of these executives is deplorable," she said, "but, perhaps, if they assumed a more manly and independent attitude, they'd receive still less support, even from the State."

"At least, that's the excuse they fling at you," he said with a shrug.

The hall matron peeped in the door and said, sleepily:

"I'm sorry, but callin' time's up!"

He regarded his wrist watch and said, "Well, I guess we'll have to say goodnight."

He arose and Ellen followed him to the door.

When she had told him goodnight, Ellen hurried down the hall to her room. She shuddered at the thought of trying to remain at Avon College without him.

At this hour of the night, Madge was usually sprawled in her bed, lost in the pages of some love story magazine. Tonight, Ellen found her bed empty, and knew that the carefree girl was probably off the campus. Just like Madge, she thought to herself, no inhibitions; no cares whatever—apparently.

Later, Ellen closed a book and looked at the clock. She saw that the hour was late. As she undressed to get in bed, she wondered if Madge would get in this time before daylight. Probably not, she thought.

CHAPTER TWELVE

Ellen awoke, the following morning feeling grateful that it was Saturday—a day of leisure, with no classes to teach. She sat up and looked across the room to the slumbering figure of Madge in the opposite bed. She had not heard Madge come in, but she was certain that she had eased in at some wee hour of the morning. Silently, she studied Madge as she slept; noted the dark lids of her closed eyes, the purplish rings about them that hinted of dissipation. Despite this, she thought that the sleeping girl's face was pretty and exotic beneath the cloud of dark, touseled hair on the pillow.

Suddenly Madge's eyes flew open and their frightened glare rested upon Ellen.

"Oh, Ellen, you scared me!" she said nervously. "That awful stare of yours! What in the world could you be thinking about me?"

"Oh, Madge, dear, pardon me! I didn't mean to

disturb you," Ellen apologized. "I was just wondering what time you got in last night."

Madge yawned wearily.

"Around three this morning," she said, smiling.

"Where on earth could you have spent the night?" Ellen said, after a gasp.

"On a little spree, for a change," Madge replied, hoarsely.

"But, how did you get by the Matron?" the other wanted to know.

"Oh, easily enough," Madge said with a flourish of her hands. "You see, Gail Hinds put me next to her. You know Gail Hinds, the near-white senior kid whose dad, they say, is a wealthy white man in Braxton?—"

"Yes," Ellen said, "I know her. She's the one we said could easily be attending the State University, passing for white."

"Well," Madge went on, "she's a real sport! She put me wise to the matron. She stands good with her. We bribed the old heifer with a dollar, and she let us out with the instruction to have a good time and be in before daybreak—for her own protection, you know."

Ellen was shocked by this information about the matron.

"Madge," she said, "do you mean to tell me that the matron would—"

"Hell, yes!" Madge cut her short. "She'll do anything for money. She's pretty tight on most of the students, because they're too poor to bribe her, but she's 'peaches' with Gail, because Gail handles money and stands in with several of these white officials who come out here, especially with Gill. I gave Gail a thorough trouncing for not putting me next to the old hussy sooner. I thought of all the thrills I've missed by not knowing the trick before now."

"But, Madge, you can't afford it!" Ellen said sharply, then added, solicitously, "you can't jeopardize your standing by taking such chances with this Gail Hines and her white men friends!"

"Oh, there you go with your dam' presumptions!" Madge commented angrily. "Why didn't you wait 'til I said we were with her white men friends? Well, you presumed correctly this time. We kept a 'date' with Gill and a friend of his in Braxton. Jesse Sales drove us to meet 'em, in his car. Of course, he took no further part in the party. He's great on 'date'-making for these whites—just another reason why he wields such a big stick around here. I guess there's nothing too low for him to do for 'em."

"Madge, you don't seem to understand," Ellen said pleadingly. "I'm more interested in you than you think. I don't wish to believe that you are a bad woman, Madge. Associating with white men, down here, is considered one of the lowest things a colored woman can do." The tone of her voice revealed her keen disappointment in the other whom she had come to love so much. "Oh, Madge," she begged in despair, "what happened? Did you do anything wrong?"

Madge did not answer her immediately; just sat upright in the bed, staring down at the billowing cover about her.

In her new appraisal of Madge, Ellen, of course, did not take into consideration that girl's background, nor that of any of Madge's relatives. She did not know that neither Madge's parents, nor their parents before them, had ever lived in the South. She did not know that Madge's association with whites, all her life, had been without the inhibitions on the inter-racial question with which she herself had been brought up. She did not think of it at this moment, but it was true that her own grandparents had been migrants to th North; hence, their inhibitions had come down from them to herself.

"Now, Ellen," Madge said presently, "just stay in your teddies! Nothing happened to me, except that the drinks were pretty peppy. All four of us got a little 'tight,' but that was all. They carried us to a colored woman's house over there, and we played a little poker 'til we got too 'tight.' Naturally, the men petted us a bit, but they went no further. I can protect myself, you know."

"I don't mean to meddle, Madge," Ellen said wistfully, "but when I see you headed wrong—well, I can't be silent. It's so different down here to what it is where you're from. White men down here don't mean any good toward colored women when it comes to socializing with them. It may sound prudish to you, but I'm afraid for you to repeat the spree you went on last night."

Somehow, Madge was convinced that Ellen spoke the truth, but she hated to admit it.

"Well, what the hell is a woman to do around here for a change?" she wanted to know. "Surely, you've never had a forbidden thrill, Ellen!" she went on, "for if you had, it seems to me you'd see my point. What chance have we for romance here in this prison? We're watched and guarded as if we were wild animals!"

"Why, there are men on the faculty here who'd be glad of your attention, Madge—colored men! Why not go with one of them?"

Madge laughed scornfully.

"Yes, I know!" she said. "Now, wouldn't I look—dragging around here with one of these spineless faculty sissies? I haven't met a single one that could interest me. What do they know of romance? What sort of a thrill could I get, listening to them talk about their darned work? Most of them are degree-and-fraternity mad, and I don't give a cuss about either!"

Ellen got out of her bed.

"Well," she said, "I wouldn't attempt to dissuade you from your choice of male-companioship, if we weren't here in the South. But, I do want you to be careful, Madge." With this, she hurried into the bathroom.

Madge rolled, stiffly, out of her bed.

"Well," she called to Ellen, "I appreciate your interest in me. At least, we won't fall out about it."

CHAPTER THIRTEEN

Christmas stole upon Avon College almost before Ellen realized it. Down here, Christmas was not accompanied by a blanket of snow, as Ellen had always seen it at home, but it brought the same atmosphere of cheerfulness to which she had been accustomed. Many of the faculty members went home to spend the holidays, but Ellen and Madge joined those who remained on the campus.

Nothing would have pleased Ellen better than to go home to Mom and Mae, but she counted the cost and decided that the money she would have to spend to go home would do more good in Mom's purse, to pay for the necessities that must go on the year around. Another point against her going home was the fact that her male chorus was to perform for Mrs. Burt on the night of New Year's eve.

To Ellen, the week passed swifty, and the climax to months of rehearsing her male chorus was just a night off. Somehow, she dreaded it. Mrs. Burt had stopped by her room, that day, with the information that they were to appear in the banquet hall of the Hotel Gables, in Braxton, at the behest of a party of State legislators who had billed the performance of the Avon College boys as their contribution to the banquet.

Mrs. Burt's parting words to Ellen had been, "Remember, honey, we must be on time! You know, white folks believe in being on time. Dont' forget that Avon College will be on trial. We've got to do our best!"

After Mrs. Burt had gone, Ellen begged Madge to go with them to Braxton. "It'll be a nice trip for you," she said to Madge.

"No, thanks," Madge answered quickly. I wouldn't

care to be embarrased by old lady Burt. She's what they call 'a white folks' nigger.' She never tires of licking 'em. It's a wonder her old flabby chin isn't a solid corn from bowing so low to 'em. If you didn't just have to go to keep your job, I wouldn't advise you to go with that woman any place where whites are going to be. She's a regular flunkey for 'em, and in her spare time, they keep her busy making ginger cakes and rag mammy-dolls for their children. All she wants is a smile from 'em in return. No," she shrugged, "I'll stay here and, maybe, whisper a prayer for you."

"Well," Ellen said, "I'm only to sit at the piano and accompany the boys' singing, and when we're through with the numbers, I suppose we'll have nothing to do but leave. I hope so, anyway."

"Just you be prepared for the worst," Madge warned. "By the time you get a dozen requests to play 'Swing Low Sweet Chariot' and 'Ain't Gonna Study War No Mo,' " by some black-mammy-reared 'cracker," you'll be good and ready to leave, all right."

For the moment, Ellen was severely conscious of the humiliation which Madge predicted for her, but, as the hours passed, she thoroughly resigned herself to whatever tonight held for her. Later, she hurried to the conservatory for a last minute rehearsal with the boys.

During the rehearsal, she felt as if she would never again hold the plaintive Negro spirituals and jubilees in her heart as music worthy of veneration. In her ears, their subtle minor notes debased themselves to miserable groans of pain and dejection.

At last came the hour of departure for Braxton. Ellen and Mrs. Burt and the group of young men climbed into the big college bus, at the administration building, and were off. Ellen sat next to Mrs. Burt.

Mrs. Burt was anxious and talkative.

"Now, honey," she cautioned her, "you want to do your best tonight. You see, these white folks like Negro music with plenty of pep in it. That makes 'em know we're grateful for the money they've put behind the college. If we make 'em feel good, we'll get that new building right away."

"I intend to do my best," Ellen promised. "The boys sing exceptionally well, so I'm not uneasy.

"That's the spirit!" Mrs. Burt said, nodding briskly.

Almost before Ellen realized it, the bus was coming to a halt in an alley which skirted the rear of the Hotel Gables. Thoughtlessly, she stepped down out of the bus and started up the alley toward the front of the hotel.

"Come back!" Mrs. Burt called to her, "colored folks have to go in the side door here!" Then she beckoned frantically to the young men. "Hurry boys," she urged them, "we can't have them waiting on us!"

Inside the building, the party stopped at a passenger elevator shaft, and Mrs. Burt pressed a button. In stantly, the elevator dropped to their level, and with an impatient frown, the white operator sleepily opened the door. He was angered when he saw that his prospective passengers were not of his own hue.

"Y'all don't want up in this car!" he drawled harshly and authoritatively, indicating with his finger an open freight lift in the rear of the room. "If you niggers want to go up, git back yonder to that baggage lift!" he added, his anger flaming by this time.

"Thank y'sir," Mrs. Burt said, bowing low to him. "Come this way," she said to Ellen and the young men, "We go up back here. Lord, I believe we're late!"

The plainly outraged white man on the baggage lift shot them upward recklessly and herded them off on a floor that was in darkness. After stumbling about cautiously, they pushed through a swinging door and found themselves behind the stage of the banquet hall. A tiny electric light bulb furnished all the illumination they had. The black curtain of the stage separated them from a full room of whites out front.

Presently, a burly white man, with a red and scowling face, stepped through the back curtain of the stage and faced them. He wore black broadcloth and his coat was frocked. He was Mr. Slimp, the master of ceremonies.

"Well, here we are, Mr. Slimp," Mrs. Burt announced, grinning broadly.

The white man gruffly ignored her greeting.

"Come on! come on! you're late!" he said. To the others, including Ellen, he ordered, "Get lined up an' wait 'til I announce you, then come on the stage an' give 'em all you got. Make it good and spicy! Strictly jubilees and spirituals. Don't attempt any white folks music; we've already had plenty of that." His instructions to them finished, he stepped back through the curtain on the stage.

Ellen and her party could hear his gruff voice as he talked to the audience before him. She winced at his every biting word.

"Now, good people," she heard him concluding, "last, but in no-wise least, you are to listen to my niggers from Avon College, the nigger State school that your money provides for 'em. They're going to sing you some good old spirituals and jubilees! I want you to know that the few dollars in taxes you pay for the support of this school ain't wasted! You see, we're trainin' these niggers to be cooks, brick-layers, tillers of the soil, and the like. We ain't trainin' 'em to be 'ladies and gentlemen!' We leave that job for the Yankee schools up north!" Vociferous applause followed this from him.

As he went on with his insulting introduction, Ellen felt herself weakening, and knew that Mrs. Burt's eyes were following her as she leaned wearily against a nearby post.

Mrs. Burt moved closer to her.

"Now, honey," she apologized, "don't pay no attention to what he says. He means no harm."

"No—no harm?" the heartsick girl articulated. "Why, Mrs. Burt, I'm sick! I—I don't believe I—"

"But you must go through with this!" Mrs. Burt cut her short. "Pull yourself together! Do you realize your job depends on how you make it here tonight?" Mrs.

Burt waited for no answer from Ellen, but turned from her and busied herself in getting the young men lined up for the stage.

The voice of the master of ceremonies was triumphant.

"Now, here they come!" he shouted to his audience— "Your and my nigger boys from Avon College!" With this, he thrust his head through the curtain and nodded, impatiently, to Mrs. Burt.

"Let 'em come, Sally!" he ordered.

"Yessir, Mr. Slimp!" Mrs. Burt answered him, then nudged Ellen: "Go on, now! Sit down at the piano and play your best!" she whispered to her huskily.

How the young men got on the stage, and how she herself made it to the piano, Ellen never afterward knew. All she was to remember was the raucus applause the whites gave them after each selection.

She did not return to herself until she was again in the bus, on the way back to Avon College. She sat beside Mrs. Burt and wept softly, from nervous exhaustion.

"Now, you mustn't do that!" Mrs. Burt said to her rebukingly. "You and the boys did well tonight. You see, you must forget your pride, if you are to make good at Avon. As the director of music, you've got to be a good mixer."

"But, Mrs. Burt," Ellen sobbed, "such as this is more than I can stand! Perhaps, I'm the wrong one for this position. Why, I'll never forget this horrible night!"

Mrs. Burt stared at her with an expression of disgust.

"Young woman," she began hotly, "you're acting plain foolish! Why, them very white folks make it possible for you and all the rest of us colored folks to have jobs. You may as well get used to it, if you've got to work for a living. There's no teaching jobs for you up North, so you'd just as well adjust yourself to conditions down here!"

"I've tried hard to adjust myself, Mrs. Burt, but I can't! I can't!" Ellen cried hysterically.

"But you must!" Mrs. Burt shouted angrily. "You will, if you stay at Avon! You're no better than I am, and I've been at Avon a good many years!"

Ellen did not answer the older woman, but wished that she could scream at her with all her might. Suddenly, she hated her; hated the Southland, and even the teaching profession. For the moment, she hated everything!

CHAPTER FOURTEEN

Winter passed on, and early spring bestowed a mantle of delicate blossoms upon the campus of Avon College and the country surrounding. The out-of-doors was a floral riot of color, from the delicate tint of blue-bonnets and wild roses to the creamy white of fragrant magnolia blossoms in the trees.

As she went to and fro, on the campus, in attendance upon her duties, Ellen breathed the refreshing, scented air in zestful draughts. One thing, she thought, nature observed no color line in the distribution of her glorious gifts over the Southland. Indeed, she must have paused at Avon College for an extra wave of her magic wand, for now, the campus was a veritable Garden of Eden.

It was the season for tennis, and each evening, faculty-devotees of the sport strolled out to the courts and exercised muscles that the winter months had left soft and flabby. The paths of romance—such romance as could be indulged in out in the open—were those that led to and from the tennis courts. For some inexplicable reason, the taut rules of discipline that governed affairs-of-the-heart at Avon College slackened slightly on the tennis courts. Hence, few evenings passed that did not witness matches between Ellen and Dewalt. When not tripping behind the balls on a court, they sat together on the low-hung bleachers and talked.

They were sitting on the bleachers that evening when Jesse Sales drove up in his car. He alighted on the grass,

at some distance from where they sat, and beckoned to
Dewalt. Dewalt excused himself from her, and strode
over to where Sales stood.

Ellen felt, intuitively, that all was not well between
them. Her puzzlement was of short duration, however,
for she could hear their words plainly.

"Well, Brooks," she heard Sales say to him impudently, "I let you get by on the membership dues you
should've paid to the State Teachers Association, last
fall; even though you were the only one that didn't pay
that three dollars. You got by 'cause I felt that a racket
with you might injure the morale of the other faculty
members that willingly paid it—"

"Very few of them willingly paid it!" Dewalt cut him
short. "They paid it because they were afraid not to!
Do you realize that?" Dewalt's tone was suddenly arro-
gant.

Sales evaded his question:

"Brooks, you're not in accord with the administration!" he shot. "As the newly elected president of the
Association, Principal Johns was deserving of all our support, which would have been a hundred percent had you
fell in line with the rest of the teachers."

"The Principal coerced the faculty with the threat of
taking their jobs from them, and I simply refused to be
coerced by his threats," Dewalt explained. "I hold to
the same principle today!" he added hotly.

Sales set one foot on the fender of his car, and his gold
teeth glittered through a smirkish slit of a grin.

"Well," he said, "that's not what I want with you now.
I completed an inventory of your classroom stock yesterday, and found about fifteen dollars worth of practice
material missing. I stopped by to tell you I'm holding
up your next salary check for that amount. You'll certainly pay that!"

"Huh!" Dewalt laughed derisively. "So, you intend
to get even with me that way! Well, you're mistaken.
I've never carried a supply of material that large in my

classroom. There's no room in there for that much material. I've been securing it from the warehouse, just as we need it. If material for my department is missing, the warehouse is responsible for it!"

Sales' anger flamed.

"I'm holding you responsible for it!" he shouted to the other. "Don't think, for a moment, I'm gonna let you cheat the State like you cheated the Teachers Association! I—" Sales got no further. The sudden impact of Dewalt's fist against his jaw, sent him reeling to the ground. For a second, he lay inert, then he staggered to his feet, and with clenched jaws, advanced a step toward his adversary. But Dewalt propped himself to deliver another blow.

During the tense interval, Ellen dashed from the bleachers and stepped between the two angry men.

"Please don't!" she cried, clinging to Dewalt's arm.

Taking advantage of this respite, Sales turned dazedly and got into his car. Without another word, he drove out of the crowd which had gathered about them.

"How dare you, Dewalt!" Ellen said to him rebukingly. "Why, it may mean that we'll have to separate!" she added, a lump forming in her throat.

Chagrin was now taking the place of his anger.

"I'm sorry, Ellen—because of you," he said, "but he called me a cheat, and I simply couldn't take it. Others drop their heads and take that dirty tyrant's abuses, but I can't! I'd rather go back North and—and sling a mop, even!"

* * *

After he had left her on the campus, Ellen did not go into her dormitory. Near it was a stone bench under a magnolia tree. She sat down on it and marveled at the fragrant odor of the blossoms in the tree. Dusk settled over the countryside and lulled her into a solitary reverie. Across the eastern expanse of prairie, the shrill whistle of the North-bound evening train pierced the scented atmosphere, sending a chill through her heart, as she imagined that one evening, very soon, perhaps, Dewalt Brooks, the one and only man in her life, might be on that train, leaving her alone with only fond memories and uncertain hopes. She wished that she, too, could soon be leaving. What could this place mean to her without him? she wondered. This place! she thought. Why, it was no more than an inferno of prejudice and hate! She tried to recall something she had once read, and its author might well have been referring to Avon College. Was it from "Dante's Inferno?" she wondered, or in what had she read it? "Abandon hope all you who enter here!"—it read something like that, she thought to herself with a chuckle.

Repeated taps of the evening campus bell brought her back to earth, and she arose and hurried to her dormitory. She saw immediately that Madge had been to the room, dressed and gone. The abandon with which that girl's athletic clothes were scattered about the room was mute and convincing testimony of this. There were that girl's white middy blouse and black bloomers, draping the back of a chair, and in the middle of the floor were her white canvas shoes, stuffed with black-ribbed stockings. Ellen reflected: Just like Madge—so awfully slouchy indoors, yet so tastefully neat outside. Downright carelessness!

Still, she envied Madge's light-heartedness—her utter freedom from worry, regardless of what happened.

"She's about on another spree tonight," Ellen guessed audibly, as she gathered up the abandoned clothes and hung them in the closet. She saw that Madge's chic spring coat was missing from the closet, and knew by this that Madge must be off the campus.

When Ellen had wearily dragged herself to bed, she could not sleep; instead, the events of the day trailed one another through her mind, halting at the altercation between Dewalt and Jesse Sales. Despite her effort to shut it out of her mind, the entire incident, word for word and movement for movement, reenacted itself before her. Only the menacing whine of the wind outside, and the distant roar of thunder, divorced Dewalt and his unfortunate affair from her mind. Momentarily, darts of lightning slashed the darkness, and she soon realized that another storm was gathering, which, any minute now, would be drenching the country-side with its raging fury of water. She shuddered for Madge. Off the campus and a storm coming!

Suddenly, rain and hail begain beating a tatoo on the window panes, so intensifying her uneasiness for Madge that she could lie in bed no longer. She got up, stuck her tiny feet into mules, and hastened to the window, not taking the time to turn on the light. She peered out through the blinding rain as darts of lightning played about her slender form. A glance at the luminous face of the clock on the dresser revealed the hour to be two o'clock.

"Dear God, please take care of her!" she whispered prayerfully.

Presently, she heard Madge's key turn in the door latch. As Madge staggered in, she snapped on the light.

Ellen was wholly unprepared for the sight which faced her.

"Madge!" she gasped to the wet, bedraggled girl standing before her.

Madge was completely exhausted, and the stare from her bloodshot eyes was vacant.

"It's me, or what's left of me!" she said hoarsely.

Frantically, Ellen rushed to her.

"Oh, Madge!—Madge, what's happened to you?" she cried. "Where on earth have you been?" She followed the disheveled girl to her bed.

For a minute Madge did not answer her; instead, she sat down on her bed and cupped her chin in her hands, then breathed more easily. The low-cut dress she wore revealed several scratches and bruises on her well-formed shoulders.

Finally Madge answered her, brokenly, as if intoxicated:

"Been everywhere!" she cried. "Been doing everything! Gill! Gill's had me—all night!—big time with him!" The nauseating smell of liquor escaped on her breath.

For moments, Ellen was speechless and trying to swallow the lump which had risen in her throat. She loved Madge, in sort of a motherly fashion, and this sight of the once lovely girl, now suddenly transformed into a drunken hag, stunned her.

"Madge, this is horrible!" she exclaimed at last. "You've been mistreated! That dirty white man has—has—oh, what would your mother think, if—"

"Oh, Ellen! please! Mother mustn't know this!" Madge sobbed piteously.

Ellen sat down beside her, threw her trembling arms about her and kissed her tenderly, tearfully.

"Now, now, darling," Ellen began sympathetically, "your mother shan't know about this. I'll help you all I can. Come, let's get these wet clothes off. A warm bath will help you."

Hurriedly, Ellen unfastened the weakened girl's clothes and stripped them from her flushed body. Then she hastened to the bathroom and returned with a bowl of warm water into which she had poured a measure of camphor. Tenderly, she bathed the feverish face and body, then assisted the now recuperating girl into a negligee of soft material.

"Ellen," Madge began in a calmer voice, "darling, you're an angel to me! I'm ashamed of myself! Whatever comes of this, will you promise you won't tell mother, Ellen?" She began sobbing bitterly.

"Darling, I promise she'll never know," Ellen assured her. "There now, get in bed. You'll be all right tomorrow."

After tucking the sobbing, penitent girl in bed, Ellen turned out the light and dragged her spent body into her own bed. Silently, she shared the same anguish that reduced Madge to a weeping, helpless child. Copious tears drenched her own pillow as she sought relaxation beneath the downy folds of the cover. What would be the after effect of this latest escapade of Madge's? she wondered.

CHAPTER FIFTEEN

Ellen dressed on tiptoe, that next morning, for she did not wish to arouse Madge from a much needed sleep. She was just about to leave the room when Madge stirred nervously and opened her dark, swollen eyelids.

"How do you feel, dear?" Ellen wanted to know.

The other yawned wearily and stretched her throbbing limbs.

"Oh," she said, "I'm stiff, got a crackling headache and feel like an old woman!"

"Well," Ellen said, 'that calls for more rest. I think you should stay in bed all day. Suppose you do just that?" she added thoughtfully.

Suddenly, a pitiful expression flickered across Madge's face and she looked at Ellen seriously.

"I will, if you say so," she answered, then, "Ellen, will you forgive me for what I did last night?"

"Of course I forgive you, Madge," Ellen told her. "You haven't done me so much harm as you've done yourself."

Presently, tears rose in Madge's eyes and she swallowed and blinked to keep them back.

"Ellen, I'm uneasy about myself," she said, low and gravely. "You know, they made me awfully drunk—doped me or something. I don't remember what happened next, until I came in this morning." She dropped her eyes and shook her head slowly. "Oh, I'm not naturally bad, Ellen, but—well, it's just this place! One simply has to do something once in a while to break the awful monotony."

"Yes, this place is terribly depressing," Ellen confirmed, "In a way," she went on, "slavery still exists on this old plantation, but we musn't let it get hold of us and make us do things that are detrimental to us."

Madge's tears had receded, and her voice carried a note of irony.

"Slavery is the word!" she said, "and the only difference between this and that of the past is that the faculty members are the slaves, and Jesse Sales and Obadiah Johns are the overseers—and no 'Simon Legree' was ever harder."

"Well," Ellen suggested solicitously, "you'd better not brood over the situation now. You're in need of more rest. I'll have your breakfast sent from the cafeteria, then I'll report your illness to the Principal."

* * *

Deep within herself, Ellen sat down at a table in the cafeteria. She realized that life's problems were now falling upon her, one after the other, and she wondered if a climax—a turning point in her career—was near at hand. It was as if something dreadful was closing in upon her. She thought of her salary checks and what they meant for Mom and Mae. No, she thought, she must not lose her position! Half-heartedly, she gave the student-waiter her order—grapefruit, black coffee, toast and butter.

"Double that order, waiter!" Dewalt Brooks called to the waiter from behind her. He came around and sat down at the table opposite her. "How are you this morning?" he said to her.

"Oh, I'm a little depressed," she answered, then added, "How are you?" Quickly she noted the expression of futility on his face.

"The same here!" he said drily. "And I'm about to do something about it," he added.

She looked at him again, this time curiously.

"Just what do you mean?" she said.

Nervously, he raised his elbows to the table, cradled his chin between his fists and looked her in the face intently.

"I'm handing in my resignation today," he said deliberately.

"You mean to say that you're—you're resigning?" she asked, a note of despair in her voice.

He nodded slowly.

"That's right," he said, "I'm leaving. I guess I'll go back to Chicago, or to some other place where I may find something to do."

Ellen was stunned for the moment, and her lips twitched slightly at the thought of possibly losing him.

"B-But, there's nothing to employ your training in that direction," she said at last.

"That's true," he said, "but I intend to take anything I can find; bell-hopping, portering, anything!" he shrugged.

"Well," she went on slowly, "it's not that I blame you for wishing to get out of this sort of an existence, but— oh, Dewalt, I'll be so lonely without you!" She felt a dreadful tightening about her heart.

He swallowed audibly before he spoke, then, philosophically:

"Well, such seems to be this sort of life—acquaintance, love, then, farewell. Ellen," he went on gravely, "maybe I shouldn't ask you to wait for me, but, whatever happens, I'll go on loving you always. Will you do the same?"

She yearned to recline in his arms and sob—unleash the deep love for him that swirled about her heart like the turbulent waters of a river, but she reasoned that she must control herself and not appear weak to him.

"Yes," she said softly, "I will." Then, looking pleadingly into his eyes, "Please believe me, Dewalt!" she whispered.

Later in the day, Ellen found time to reflect upon the situation. In a day or two, she thought, Dewalt would be going, perhaps out of her life forever. There was Madge—she loved her, too—but there was no telling about what the impulsive Madge was likely to do. As a matter of fact, she felt strangely apprehensive about Madge, since that girl's wild escapade the night before. Save for Madge, she would be utterly alone at Avon College, now. The majority on the faculty were decidedly Southern, and they seemed to possess sectional prejudice to a glaring fault. Her own gestures at friendliness with them had been. time after time, turned away with icy coldness.

"Only if I could take this life here as Madge takes it!" she said to herself wistfully, knowing, the while, that she could never assume Madge's attitude about things.

"You're a hell of a reliable person to trust one's affairs with!" Madge told her angrily, that evening, after she returned to the room from the conservatory. Madge deliberately threw an opened letter at her feet. "Take a look at that letter from 'Uncle Obe'!" she added hotly.

Stunned, Ellen nervously picked up the letter and read it.

The letter said:

"Miss Conley: meet me at my office in the morning at eight o'clock, and explain why you missed your classes today. Also, be prepared to explain why you were off the campus so late last night, and with whom."

Done reading the letter, Ellen's heart ached as she stood fingering it and searching for words to explain.

Finally, she said: "I'm sorry, Madge, but I forgot to go by and make an excuse for you. I—well—"

"Cut the dam' explanation!" Madge flamed. "You've simply messed me up, that's all! Now, I've got to do some unnecessary explaining to that ignorant old jackass!"

Guiltily, Ellen was wondering just how she had managed to forget.

"I—I know it's awful, Madge," she said, "and I'll do anything to help you out of it."

"Well, I reckon you should!" Madge said sternly. "Perhaps, if you had gone by this morning, he wouldn't've investigated and learned that I was off the campus last night. Well, you can go with me tomorrow and help me to explain."

Ellen nodded meekly.

"I'll go with you," she said. "I understand," she added, "that he's awfully contemptible to one called in on a charge. I hope you'll control your temper, Madge."

"I'll try to," Madge replied, "but I don't intend to be bluffed and insulted by him. I'll tell the truth, and won't bite my tongue in doing it!"

"You mean," Ellen said, "that you'll tell him whom you were out with last night? You're not going to tell him you were out with—with—"

"With Gill!" Madge supplied. "Of course I am! Why should I lie about it? The worst he can do is to discharge me—and maybe he won't do that when I'm through telling everything!"

Long after Madge was asleep, and Avon College was quiet, Ellen stirred in bed, sleeplessly. She wondered how Madge could sleep so peacefully in the face of the ordeal which the approaching morning held for her. One thing, she thought, Madge was courageous and honest. Madge had said that she would tell the truth, and Ellen knew that she would do just that.

CHAPTER SIXTEEN

Ellen tired of her bed long before daybreak. After what to her seemed an eternity, morning came. She waited for Madge to arouse from a quiet, peaceful sleep, but that girl did not stir until Ellen got out of her own bed and shook her vigorously.

Madge got up feebly and sat on the side of her bed, her chin cupped in her hands.

"Thank you, darling," she rewarded Ellen for awakening her, then, with a sigh, "you're like a mother to me, Ellen. You know, I feel strangely uneasy—as if something terrible threatens me—" she paused and shivered slightly, then burst into unrestrained tears. "Ellen!" she cried "I'm afraid!"

Ellen laid a comforting hand on the sobbing girl's shoulder.

"But, Madge, it's not like you to be upset like this. The worst the Principal would dare to do is to discharge you—"

The other stopped crying and looked at Ellen seriously.

"It's something more serious than meeting Johns this morning;" she said, "something—I don't know what it is —I've never been up against before."

Ellen was frankly puzzled.

"Well, I wonder what on earth could it be?" she said uneasily.

"Maybe—" the other paused again, then, "oh, Ellen, I haven't the courage to tell you what something tells me it might be, but—well, I'll not be a coward any longer!" Her features hardened and a gleam of courage took the place of fear in her eyes. "Whatever happens," she went on, "I'm going to stay here and fight for all I'm worth! I won't be driven away! I'll stay right here and see the dam' thing through!"

* * *

At eight o'clock that morning, the two girls were admitted into the private office of Principal Johns. He did not rise, but motioned them to chairs facing him.

Madge cooly proffered him the letter she had received from him the day before.

"I'm here in answer to this," she said nonchalantly.

"Uh huh!" he mumbled, taking the letter. "Well," he said calculatingly, "you're gonna tell me you missed

yesterday 'cause you was ill.   I'm used to that ol' excuse.   But, that ain't the main thing I want to see you
'bout—" he paused and pulled out a drawer of his desk
from which he withdrew a yellow sheet"—this is a dismissal sheet, an' I'm debatin' in my mind whether to fill
it out for you this mornin'!   You was out spreein' 'round
with some man night befo' las,' an' that ain't the first
time.   Now, I want to know who 'twas an' what y'all did!
Out with it!"

Madge looked at him silently and sarcastically before
she spoke, then:

"When I tell you whom I was with, maybe you'd
rather not know!"

Instantly Johns flamed at her sarcasm.

"Now, young woman, I'm not havin' no sass outa you,
d'you undertand?   Avon College ain't no place for ras-
cals and harlots!"

This from him brought Madge suddenly to her feet
and she stood over him threateningly:

"Don't you dare say it again, you goddam' liar!" she
screamed.   "I won't take it!   I'm not a harlot!"

Johns sprang to his feet and gesticulated wildly:

"Get back to your room and pack your trunk!" he
roared.

A sneering grin now shadowed Madge's crimson face.

"But, not before I inform you that night before last,
and other nights, I was out with your general manager,
Gill.   Your treasurer, Sales, always helps him plan our
dates!" she laughed smirkishly.

Johns' lower lip dropped and he sank into his chair as
if stricken.   For the moment, he sat utterly speechless.

Ellen placed a restraining hand on Madge's arm, but
Madge went on, derisively, "I don't mind leaving, old
man, nor do I mind airing everything I know, if I must
leave!   The Negro press will be glad to get some inside
dope about this place.   This under-cover mixing of the
races here, with certain of you Negro officials acting as
'go-betweens,' would make a nice, interesting story.   Per-

haps a little story about the relations between a certain girl-student and a prominent State legislator's son will make good 'front-page' for about three hundred newspapers."

At last Johns summoned utterance:

"Now, Miss Vance," he said sheepishly, "I—well there ain't no use to broadcast scandal 'bout this place. We must think of all these poor students! You—you—" he paused nervously.

"I stay on, then!" she supplied quickly.

With nervous fingers, he beat a tatoo on his desk. Then, thoughtfully, he slowly nodded his bald head.

"Better that than scandal, I s'pose," he said in gruff resignation.

"All right, then!" she said to him, then to Ellen who stood beside her, "we'll be going to our room, then!"

Together, they walked out of Johns' office, leaving him limp in his chair, as if he had just awakened from a fearful nightmare.

Madge laughed wildly and victoriously as they entered their room.

"I guess the whip's in my hand now!" she cried to Ellen.

"It's—It's really awful, Madge," Ellen said deploringly. "I—mean, the circumstances. Maybe, after all, you'd do better to go away and forget this place." To herself, she was thinking: "From now on, she'll not be here because of her ability, but because of their fear of exposure by her."

"Perhaps you're right, Ellen," Madge replied, more seriously, "but there's a greater force to consider: Nature! It all depends on what step Nature chooses to take."

Ellen did not comment. She just looked at her roommate intently and wondered what she meant.

"You're wondering what I mean, aren't you?" Madge said huskily.

Ellen nodded slowly. "Yes," she murmured.

"I simply mean that—I—," Madge paused, shudder-ingly— "oh, well," she said, a little chokingly, "maybe things will turn out all right!" She told herself that she simply hadn't the nerve to tell Ellen what was in her mind.

Ellen pushed her for no further explanation.

CHAPTER SEVENTEEN

Ellen was thankful that Avon College boasted a library. It was nothing to compare with the one at her Alma Mater, but what she managed to pick, in the way of books, from its spare shelves did much toward lessen-ing the monotony about her.

A week had passed since she witnessed Madge's verbal tilt with the Principal, and tonight, she sat lost in the pages of a book. Madge lay on her bed absorbed in the usual love story magazine, and frowned impatiently when Ellen hurried across the room to answer an impulsive knock at the door.

She greeted Gail Hinds at the door. Gail said "hello" and brushed past her to Madge. Ellen wondered what silly student-gossip the girl was bringing Madge this time. Just like Madge to be so familiar with a student, she thought.

Madge laid her magazine aside—she was never too absorbed in anything for a chat with Gail—and sat up on her bed.

"How's everything, Gail?" she greeted the visitor expectantly, noting the angry crimson flush on Gail's white face.

Unbidden, Gail dropped down on the side of Madge's bed before she answered, then, "Everythings bum with me!" she said.

Madge's smile vanished.

"What now?" she said, regarding the angry girl seriously.

"I'm around to say goodbye," Gail told her. "They're sending me home tomorrow!"

"Gail!" Madge cried, "sending you home? What've you done, now?"

"No more than what I've been doing all the time," Gail said. "I was out with Ellery Perry a night or two ago," she added.

"Ellery Perry?" Ellen, who had until now been silent, said with a gasp, "why, isn't he—"

"Yes, he's white!" Gail answered quickly. "Dean Warren—the grisly old cat!—she's had me expelled!"

Madge laughed disgustedly.

"So, I guess she's decided to 'clean up' the place, starting with the smartest and best looking student on the campus," she said.

"They say she was at the bottom of your trouble, too, Madge," Gail informed. "It's mighty funny how she's permitted all kinds of dirt to go on here 'til since she's heard about you and me and our white 'crushes.' Now, she's trying to burst out of her flannels!"

"Well, I'm not the least bit alarmed," Madge boasted, "for I've got the whip in my hand, now, so far as my affairs are concerned. She's laying off me from now on! Take my word for it, kid!"

"I don't mind going home at all," Gail went on, "for I'm sick of this place anyhow. But, she's already stuck herself a little too far into the affairs of these whites, I'm thinking. If she knew what I know, she'd be getting away from here herself," She nodded vigorously, and knowingly. "She'd better look out!" she warned.

Ellen gasped.

"Just what do you mean? Is she in danger?" she interrupted their conversation.

Gail got up from where she was sitting on Madge's bed.

"Just you two keep your eyes open!" she suggested. "Well," she added, "I'm saying so-long. Might be back next year." She extended her small white hand to Ellen.

"So-long, Gail," Ellen said. "I do hope you'll make it back next year."

By this time, the thought of parting with Gail had moved Madge to tears. She got out of bed and threw her arms around the almost white girl.

"So-long, Gail," she said sobbingly, "I know I'll be missing you terribly, darling!"

The impulsive Gail bit her lips in an effort to restrain the tears that finally trickled down her cheeks.

"So-long, Madge," she said chokingly, "I'll be seeing you next year, if—if you're here." With this, she turned quickly and hurried out of the room from them, slamming the door behind her.

Ellen returned to her book, leaving Madge staring, a little nonplussed, at the closed door.

* * *

A week later, an eventful dawn enveloped the campus of Avon College. It was a Saturday, and Ellen and Madge lay awake wondering why the girls who scrubbed the bathrooms and halls, went about their work in such unusual silence. Scrub buckets being shoved over tiled floors made the only sounds that they heard.

Madge sat up in bed and stretched, shielding a wide yawn with her hand.

"Jesus, but they're quiet around here this morning!" she said. "Just like someone went about through the night and bridled their tongues," she added with a slight laugh.

"I wonder what's happened to them," Ellen said sleepily.

"Nothing, I guess," Madge vouchsafed. "Maybe," she added, "they're springing a surprise on the teachers this morning—for once this year giving us the chance to sleep off the hangover from the night before." She laughed infectuously, and Ellen joined her.

Presently, the two were hushed by a tap at the door.

"Who is it?" Madge yelled.

"Virginia!" came a voice from outside the door.

"Hell!" Madge said to Ellen who was getting up to open the door, "I wish she'd make this her last room to clean up! I'm not ready to get up yet!"

"We're still in bed," Ellen told Virginia, at the door, "would you mind coming back later to clean?"

"But, I didn't come to start cleaning," Virginia informed her. "I just stopped by to ask if y'all heard 'bout Dean Warren gettin' shot this mornin,' fore day?"

"Dean Warren, shot?" Ellen cried shrilly.

The dark brown-skinned girl did not answer immediately, for Madge, with cat-like agility, sprang out of bed and was before her, gripping her shoulders with nervous hands.

"Who shot Dean Warren, Virginia?" she cried, shaking the girl anxiously.

"Someone shot her from behin' while she was takin' her walk by the lake. They don't know who did it," Virginia replied.

Stunned, Madge turned to Ellen who was, for the moment, speechless.

"Oh, Ellen, this is terrible!" Madge cried.

Ellen did not answer her; just sat down on the side of her bed and looked at her through glassy tears. Finally, to Virginia, she said: "Is —— Is Dean Warren dead?"

"They say she's dyin' —— now," Virginia answered her brokenly, then turned abruptly and stepped out the door, closing it behind her.

"Poor Dean Warren, murdered! murdered!" Ellen murmured softly, the tears now trickling down her cheeks.

"Murdered in cold blood, Ellen!" said Madge huskily. "Poor old soul! I know she didn't deserve it!"

"But just who could have the heart to murder Dean Warren?" Ellen said vaguely. "I think she's always meant well."

"I suppose some dirty dog around here had it in for her," Madge commented, then, tense and calculating, after a thoughtful pause, " oh, I know —— I know, Ellen! Do you recall what Gail said just before she left?"

"Gail!" Ellen said, suddenly recalling that girl's ominous prediction. "Yes," she added, "I recall, now."

Madge went on: "Gail said Dean Warren had better look out —— " she paused thoughtfully, then, "why it's as plain as day who murdered her, or had her murdered —— some of these dirty low-down 'crackers', that's who!"

"Well," said Ellen, "Gail will probably know who did it. Do you think we should go to the Principal's office and report what she said?"

"Of course not!" Madge said hastily. "We know Gail herself didn't do it. If they knew what she said, they might try to hang this murder on her, to detract suspicion from these whites who, I'm certain, are in some way implicated. It's plain that they've put Dean Warren out of the way because of her efforts to stop this mixing."

"But —— but, Madge," Ellen faltered, "knowing what we do, it would be criminal to withhold it from the authorities. I'm almost sure that what we know would help them find the murderer."

"Listen, Ellen," Madge said huskily, drumming on her pillow for emphasis, "just use your head. This very moment, they have an idea that whites are behind Dean Warren's murder, and they're not anxious to have the guilty one singled out. In less than a month, the whole thing will be quashed. 'Shot by party or parties unknown', will be the verdict. Just another case like that Vinson College killing in North Carolina last year!"

Ellen dropped back on her bed limply, suddenly possessed by a feeling of guilt at the thought of withholding a possible clue to the assassination of Dean Warren.

"Well, I would feel awfully guilty to be withholding something which might help in this case."

"Now, don't be silly!" Madge rebuked her. "Telling what you know wouldn't do any good. Johns and that bunch wouldn't appreciate it. As I've said, they'll put a quietus on this thing as quick as possible. They're certain that some white man is involved, else they'd have bloodhounds out right now."

Presently, the hushed sadness which enveloped Avon College was disturbed by the tragic tolling of the campus bell. It chronicled the passing of a life —— an old custom that had come down through the years, Each resonant tap of the bell was strangely meaningful.

Dean Warren was dead!

CHAPTER EIGHTEEN

With the passing of time, the stifled hysteria which folowed the fatal shooting of Dean Nancy Warren, subsided, and though the perpetrator of the crime had not been apprehended, college activities were back to normal. As if by common agreement, all mouths of faculty officials were closed on the incident. The sudden incarceration, and later release of two male student—"suspects" were the only extent to which the law went in feigned effort to unravel the murder mystery. Obviously, this was a gesture calculated to satisfy the public that "sufficient interest" had been manifest in the effort to bring the guilty to justice.

A press release had gone out from the office of Principal Johns stating that Dean Warren had been murdered by "party, or parties unknown", but that "there will be no let-up in the search for the murderer or murderers." This statement had appeared in all the papers served by The Associated Negro Press.

Many times, Madge Conley had said to Ellen Vance, "I told you so!", and many times, Ellen had shuddered at the thought that she and Madge were, perhaps, withholding information which might lead to the immediate solution of Dean Warren's murder.

Came the evening on which Ellen said goodby to

Dewalt Brooks whose resignation had brought their romance to an abrupt close—for how long, neither had the least idea.

He looked her in the eyes, pleadingly, and murmured:

"Ellen, darling, will you wait for me?"

Breathlessly, she whispered:

"I promise, Dewalt. Always!"

Then the north-bound train took him away from her, leaving her in painful contemplation of an uncertain future without him.

That had been yesterday. But alas! no storm is ever without the sunshine in its wake! Today, Ellen received a cheery letter from her mother. She tore it open and stood reading it in the post office.

"Now, darling," Mom's letter read, "you must not be angry with me when I tell you that one month of idleness was all I could stand, so, since October, I've been manufacturing and selling my toilet preparations. I've had more than I could do; so much that I have employed six women to help me. Mae has decided to study business administration next year, so that she may manage our rapidly growing business. We finished moving into new and larger quarters yesterday. I simply couldn't hold the secret from you any longer!

Since the second month after you left, I have banked every penny you've sent me, as sort of a reserve fund—your interest in the business. Now, you're no more hampered by dependents. Hereafter, send me only what you wish me to bank for you. Save your objections 'til we meet again (smiles).

                              "Lovingly, your Mom."

"Just like Mom to do such a thing!" Ellen told herself, exultantly, as she hurried across the campus to her room. Now, she thought, she was free to pursue her own career, with no one but herself to worry about. She could be independent of her position like Madge was of

hers. Mae and Mom were independent of her! She wondered just what she would do, and how she would feel,
now that she was free to appropriate for herself every
penny that she earned, if she pleased. Finally, she decided that she would continue to let Mom bank her
money for her.

Now, she could read Dewalt's letters without a shudder at the thought of how their possible marriage might
affect those dependent upon her. Often, she had wondered just how it would feel to be free, with only one's
self to worry about. Now, she was to know!

Happily, she read Mom's letter to Madge.

"Almost too good to be true, Ellen," Madge commented. "Now you can loosen up and enjoy life without
feeling that somone else will suffer."

"But, I shan't spend any more than usual," Ellen replied. "I'll let Mom continue to bank for me, and every
extra cent will go to her for my account."

"But, you must first fix yourself up," Madge suggested, then, with calm frankness, "You need more appropriate clothes. You're a brown-skinned woman of a
beautiful type and you need clothes to emphasize your
finer points."

Ellen gasped slightly, but did not answer her immediately. She was thinking, with embarrassment: So Madge
had been considering her inappropriately dressed! She
thought of the very few things that she had to wear, and
admitted to herself that Madge was right. Momentarily, she felt that she must cry, but pride stifled her tears.

Finally, she nodded slowly, and said:

"That's true, Madge, and you've been very kind not
to tell me before. Of course, I plan to dress up."

Seeing the hurt look in the other's eyes, Madge quickly shifted the conversation:

"Well, I must be getting out to those bone-headed
students," she said, moving toward the door. "See you
later, kid!" She added, then hastened out of the room.

Alone, Ellen's thoughts drifted, for the thousandth

time, to the fate of Dean Nancy Warren. The fact that
she was withholding information of possible worth to
the case, caused her to shudder. In her mind, she again
heard the hissing prediction of Gail Hinds. In the usual
effort to stifle an accusing conscience, she reached for a
book and ploughed unsteadily through the maze of
words in it. Her eyes read them, but her mind refused
to concentrate upon them. At last, in sheer mental
exhaustion, she laid the book aside and fell across her
bed. Soon, the evening shadows were falling, and she
was asleep.

*   *   *

That night, after Madge had quit talking and fallen
asleep, Ellen lay awake, regretful that she had slept during the earlier hours of the evening, for now, in her in-
ability to go to sleep, she was exposed to the haunting
thoughts of the unsolved Warren murder. She tried
every means she knew for inducing sleep. She even
counted a thousand imaginary sheep, but to no avail.

Finally, "I can't stand it any longer!" she told herself.
She slid to the edge of the bed and sat up, blinking in the
darkness.

"Murdered in cold blood, and I withholding a possible
clue!" Her lips formed these words, but her voice failed
to utter them. Presently, she stood up, thoroughly decided that she would endure no more of this torment.
Only one way offered her relief, and she vowed, silently,
to use that way: tell what she knew!

"I'll tell what I know! —— tonight!" she said aloud,
with finality. In the darkness, she stumbled over a chair
while reaching for the light switch.

This awakened Madge:

"What th' hell?" she demanded furiously.

Before replying, Ellen flashed on the light and pulled
a garment over her tousled head. Then, through
clenched teeth:

"I'm going to see Principal Johns!" she said with determination.

Madge gasped in astonishment and raised upon her elbows, the better to see the ashen-faced girl who was now throwing on a wrap.

"What for?" Madge asked. "Don't you know he's asleep at this time of night?" she wanted to know.

"I'm going to tell him what I know about Dean Warren's murder!" Ellen snapped.

"Ellen, have you lost your mind?" Madge asked gravely. "They won't pay your story any attention. They already know who killed her! Get back into bed and forget it!"

"No!" Ellen said breathlessly, "I won't suffer any longer!" With this declaration, she snatched the door open and hurried out.

"Go ahead, then, you dam' fool!" Madge shot after her, then, to herself, "Johns will insult her! They want this thing to die down!" Then she turned her face to the wall and was soon slumbering peacefully.

*   *   *

Outside, the night was uncannily still, save for the muted roar of dynamos in the distant power plant. The ethereal stars shed a frigid glow of light across the blue-canopied heavens, and the street lights blinked here and there on the inanimate campus.

The house of Principal Johns was an aged, frame two-story affair, the largest single dwelling house on the campus. It sat behind trees, at the extreme end of a narrow ribbon pavement, north of the immediate campus.

Ellen paid no heed to the fact that the house was in complete darkness, as she entered the gate. On the front porch, she nervously rang the doorbell. After a brief interval of waiting, she heard two feet strike the floor of the front room above, and listened to them as they descended the stairs which led downward into the first floor. Somehow, she knew that those lumbering feet propelled Principal Jones.

As she stood there, her pale face sharply etched in the ray from a distant campus light, she was suddenly aware of the Principal's puzzled gaze through the glass in the door. He turned on the light, then opened the door, revealing his tall, rawboned figure garbed in a reddish, spangled bath robe. He appeared comical with a pointed night cap on his head, and the tail of his flannel nightshirt showing below the lower edges of his robe; ending several inches above his ankles which resembled huge tree knots. His long, flat feet were stuck into heelless carpet slippers.

"Well?" he said, staring at her impatiently.

Unbidden, Ellen stepped inside, past him.

"Please pardon me, Principal Johns," she said, "but it's something awfully urgent!"

"An' it just couldn't keep 'til tomorrow?" he asked.

"No!" Ellen said, "you must know it tonight!"

John's lower lip dropped, in expectation.

"Well, —— ah —— " he stammered "—wh—what is it?"

She swallowed nervously.

"It's a clue that might help in the solution of Dean Warren's murder!" she said, then added, "Gail Hinds may ——" but got no further.

"That's 'nough—that's 'nough!" he cut her short, his face distorted in a frown. "These white folks are workin' on this case, an' they know all the facts in it! They ain't got no time to run down student rumors, so ——"

"But, Principal Johns!" Ellen interrupted him protestingly, "Gail Hinds heard a threat, for she predicted, before she left, that Dean ——"

"Now, young woman," Johns broke in harshly, "nobody's called you in as a detective on this case! It'll pay you to go back to bed and stay out of it! All so-called clues is been run down, an' the case is practically settled! Jus' you get back to yo' room!" Gesturing with his long hands, he ushered her to the door. "Don't you disturb my rest like this no mo'!" he snapped.

Before she could realize it, she was stumbling out the door and it was being slammed to behind her.

"Not so much as thanks!" she murmured brokenly.

Back at the door of her room, she was conscious of intense weariness. Suddenly, she recalled that she had left her key on the inside, and the night latch was on. Now, she would have to arouse Madge to let herself in. And what thrust would Madge deal her? she wondered.

Timidly, she knocked at the door, and, presently, heard Madge hit the floor with a mutter. Madge's eyes angrily pierced her as she faced that sleepy girl in the door.

Madge was quick to detect her disappointment and dejection:

"Well, didn't I tell you?" she rasped.

"Please, Madge," Ellen said tearfully, "don't snap at me like that!"

Madge nodded her head emphatically and accusingly:

"But, didn't I tell you he'd pay you no attention?" she demanded to know.

"Yes, you did!" Ellen admitted angrily. "Now, will you let me get to bed? Please!" She brushed past the other and fell across her own bed and sobbed softly.

"You should've stayed in bed, you silly dunce!" Madge hissed at her. Ignoring the fact that Ellen had not undressed, she snapped off the light and lunged back into her bed. Later, as she slipped into her own bed; Ellen heard her fiery roommate breathing, steadily, in peaceful slumber.

CHAPTER NINETEEN

More weeks passed, drawing in their wake, the warm, smiling summer, with its session of school to which hundreds of rural and small-town school teachers had journied for the purpose of adding credits to incomplete certificates.

A small, extra bonus, supplementary to their regular salaries, was the magnet which held Ellen and Madge to their teaching posts, at the sacrifice of vacation trips home. They found the teaching of adults a far more complicated and tiresome occupation. Many of these older people had taught for years, and, often, some disgruntled student reminded them of this fact, in no uncertain terms.

Once, a buxom woman of around fifty years had seized Ellen and shook her vigorously to the accompaniment of the cutting words:

"Look here, young woman! Don't tell me I'm wrong! Why, I was teaching twenty years before you was born! I guess you're one of these little up-starts from the North, and I ain't standin' for you to try to show me up!"

Frightened out of her wits, Ellen had wrenched herself from the infuriated woman and retired to an adjoining room.

Ellen's correspondence with Dewalt Brooks had declined to the exchange of only an occasional letter, now. What was heralded as "the depression" was in full sway, and his letters reeked with pessimism. In a recent one, he said:

"Until I find something at which I can earn ample livelihood, I suppose I should not bother you with my letters. To you, I wish to be frank and truthful. If I tell the truth in them, my letters must be gloomy. To me, darling, you're a fragrant and delicate rose, and roses must have the sunshine to thrive upon. While you're not hearing from me, just know that I am searching for work. When that is found, and my letters can be full of happiness and sunshine, you will be hearing from me more often."

How silly was his philosophy! Ellen had thought with a smile. Somehow, when his letters ceased altogether, she understood, and knew intuitively that, just as surely as he had promised, he would write her again, when he was at last settled.

As if to make up for the dearth of Dewalt's letters, those from Mom and Mae increased. In one, Mom had said:

"The entire country seems to be wild over my 'La Mae'—named for our dear little Mae—toilet preparations. Many users report whitened skins and long, straight hair after only a few treatments. This will surprise you: I bought the Douglas Building on Fair Avenue last month, and it is being equipped for manufacturing on a large scale. Now, we'll be able to meet the great demand. If you've been reading the Negro newspapers, you've probably noticed the 'La Mae' advertising? Well your old Mom is behind it all. Darling, your Mom is hoping that you will not accept the teaching position for another year, as we are already independent."

Ellen had answered that, perhaps, she would come home, but suddenly awakened to the realization that now Avon College held a strange fascination for her; something which compelled yet repulsed; something akin to the deadly gleam in the eyes of a serpent with prey at bay. Perhaps that "something" which held her fascinated was merely the daily unfolding of a life so different to that which she had known before coming South.

During these hot days, Ellen had noticed a gradual change in Madge. Madge now went about as though lost in a restless dilemma; as though overshadowed by something which filled her mind with fear. The now far-away look in her once flashing eyes showed it.

*　　*　　*

One morning, Ellen returned to the room unexpectedly, just as Madge swallowed the last potion from a tiny medicine vial.

"It's medicine," Madge explained, a little guiltily. "I'm not well, Ellen," she said gravely. "Something's wrong with me. I'm afraid that — —" she hushed suddenly and dropped her troubled eyes.

Deeply touched, Ellen tried to encourage her:

"Why, you're all right," she suggested. "In fact. you seem to be gaining in weight of late. That's a good indication of robust health."

"Oh! am I?" Madge said impulsively.

Ellen regarded her up and down:

"I say you are," she confirmed.

"Oh, Ellen!" Madge cried, "I — — I wonder if it's really true that — — that I'm pregnant?" Tears were suddenly profuse on her pale cheeks, and she trembled in fear.

"Pregnant?" Ellen was shocked, but quickly regained her composure. "No!" she said. "Why, the very idea is absurd, Madge! It can't be that!" But Ellen was thinking that probably this was really the case with the other.

Madge sat down and was thoughtfully silent for several moments. Presently, she raised her eyes to Ellen, with:

"Ellen, darling — — I haven't had the courage to confide in you about my condition. I've been uncertain until this morning. That medicine was a prescription from Doctor Swanson, to hasten certain symptons, if I am pregnant, and — — and — — this morning — — this morning! Oh, Ellen, I just know it's true!" She sobbed convulsively while Ellen gazed at her, dazedly.

"But, Madge," Ellen said finally, "maybe you're wrong about the whole thing. You must be!"

Madge shook her head slowly.

"I'm not wrong, Ellen," she whispered, then, raising her voice, "but I'm staying on, whatever happens! I shan't give birth to Gill's baby! No! no! I'll die first!"

Ellen was suddenly beside her, her arms about her:

"Madge!" she said, "you're hysterical! You need rest—you've got to go to sleep!"

Suddenly, the hysterical girl was a snarling tigress, fighting at an unseen foe. She wrenched herself from Ellen's embrace and sprang to the floor, her eyes flashing.

"Sleep!" she cried, "I can't sleep! They'll order me to leave here, but I shan't go. I'll stay here and fight it through ——"

"Madge, please!" Ellen begged brokenly as tears streamed down her cheeks.

Presently, Madge got hold of herself and calmed down, her voice subsiding to something above a whisper:

"Oh, Ellen," she said, "I know you don't understand me, but I've suffered mentally, since that night the dirty white man doped me and ——" she paused, as though reliving that night, then, "oh, it's been terrible! Now, they'll want to know who the man is, and when I tell them, they'll try to make me take it back and name some colored man, but I won't lie, neither will I leave! I'm no more responsible than they are for the social condition which lead me into this trouble, so I'm staying and they can share my disgrace with me!"

"Maybe they'll help you in some way," Ellen suggested tensely.

"They must!" the other said. "I don't intend to have this baby!" she added with finality. "This evening, I'm going to Doctor Swanson, and tell him they've got help me get rid of it, else —— well, if he doesn't consent, and they order me to leave, I'll talk to the press, and I'll tell everything!"

"Well," said Ellen, "suppose you rest a bit. You'll feel better after you sleep awhile." She escorted the girl to her bed.

When she had got into the bed, Madge eyed Ellen with tender admiration.

"Ellen, you're wonderful to me!" she said. "You'll always be my friend, won't you?" she asked.

"Why, of course I will, darling," Ellen said. "There now, you sleep awhile," she added. She finished tucking the distracted girl in the bed, then went into the bathroom. There, in the closet, amid immaculate linens, she gave vent to tears.

"Yes," she said to herself, "I'll stand by her!"

* * *

Later that evening, Madge awoke from a brief sleep which strengthened her somewhat. She got up and dressed, and with Ellen, went to the Avon College Hospital.

A student-nurse seated them in the waiting room. Soon, Doctor Hugo Swanson, chief of the hospital, opened the door of his private office and regarded them. He was heavy-set and of a yellow-complexion.

"I've brought Miss Vance to sit with me during our consultation. She's my closest friend, and I've told her all," Madge told the Doctor.

Doctor Swanson eyed Ellen a little guiltily.

"Well," he said to Madge, gravely, "this is sort of unusual, but I —— I guess it's all right."

They followed the doctor into his private office, and sat down facing him.

Madge felt a little nervous under his steady gaze.

"The symptoms have appeared, Doctor," she said simply.

"Well, Miss Conley," he murmured, "that means that you'll have to be leaving the campus right away."

"No!" she objected quickly, "I don't intend to leave the campus—I intend to —— "

"Just a moment!" Doctor Swanson interrupted her. He reached for the telephone on his desk, and said to the operator: "Give me Principal Johns' residence please!"

Madge looked at him silently and rebelliously while

Ellen stirred nervously, during the moments in which the telephone connection was made.

Presently, Doctor Swanson spoke—over the telephone:

"Hello, Principal Johns," he said, "this is Doctor Swanson at the hospital. Will you come over immediately? — — Thank you."

With this, he hung up the receiver and again faced Madge:

"You understand, Miss Conley," he said, "the disposition of this case is up to Principal Johns. I talked with him about it yesterday. Now, I think it's time that we're all getting together on the next step to take."

Madge said nothing, but nodded her head. All three sat in silence until the large feet of Principal Johns shuffled to a stop at the door. Doctor Swanson got up and hastened out the door to the Principal. He closed the door behind him.

After several minutes of muted talk in the adjoining room, the two came back into the office. The doctor took his seat at his desk while Johns remained standing in the center of the floor peering over his glasses at Madge. Grasping his heavy watch chain, he came closer to her.

"Miss Conley," he addressed her, "the next best thing for you to do is to get off this campus—after you tell us what student or faculty member is guilty with you!"

Madge clenched her teeth in anger:

"No colored man is involved!" she told him. "Gill, your general manager, doped me and raped me, that night — —"

Johns caught his breath in surprise.

"Don't lie to me!" he shouted, "I know Mr. Gill —"

Madge was suddenly aflame and her eyes flashed.

"I'm not lieing!" she said. "You want me to hide this white man, but I shan't do it! Furthermore, I shan't be driven away like a dog! No!" she shook her head with finality, "I'm staying here, else I'm telling the whole story of my misfortune to the newspapers!"

For a moment, Johns stood silent, as if suddenly trans-fixed, then he spoke, this time in a kindlier tone:

"Now, Miss Conley, you must be reasonable in this matter. It simply won't do for you to stay here in a pregnant condition!"

"Neither will it do for me to go home in disgrace!" she returned coldly.

At this juncture, Doctor Swanson spoke up:

"There's a satisfactory way out of this situation," he commented, " an operation, perhaps."

Hopefully, Johns grasped at the opportunity:

"That's probably the best way!" he said to the doctor; then, to Madge, " would you submit to an operation, young woman?" Nervously, he awaited her answer.

Finally, after carefully weighing their words, she said, her voice sounding far way: "Yes, for I don't intend ever to have a baby by a white man!"

"Good!" Doctor Swanson hastened to say. "You'll have to be away from the campus only about two or three weeks then, everything'll be all right for all concerned."

Johns beamed. "All right, Doctor Swanson," he said, I'm leaving this case in your hands." With this, he strode over to the door and grasped the knob.

"Thank you, Principal Johns," Doctor Swanson said to him. "We'll be going to Braxton some time this week." He smiled pleasantly as the Principal of Avon College strode out, closing the door behind him.

Turning to Madge, Doctor Swanson said:

"Now, Miss Conley, the sooner we get at this, the better. I'll perform the operation myself. I shall arrange for Miss Vance to accompany us, if she wishes to. Could we be leaving tomorrow? The sooner, the better, you know."

The two young women stood up, and Madge staggered slightly, only to feel the reassuring support of Ellen at her side.

"Y—Yes," she answered the Doctor finally and weakly.

The two were thankful for the fresh air as they hurried across the campus to their room.

CHAPTER TWENTY

The next morning Madge and Ellen met Principal Johns and Doctor Swanson in the latter's office at the hospital. Swanson sat at his desk facing the two girls. Principal Johns remained on his feet, nervously pacing the floor.

"Miss Conley," Doctor Swanson addressed Madge, "we've arranged for you to occupy a private ward in the sanitarium of my friend, Doctor Benson of Braxton. Now, in your present condition, the operation will be a comparatively minor one. You should be completely recovered in two weeks. A private nurse of Doctor Benson's will wait on you, and it'll not be necessary for Miss Vance to stay with you the whole of that time. She can visit you two or three times a week, if she wishes."

Madge merely nodded her head gravely.

Presently, Principal Johns halted in his pace:

"Everything's been arranged to keep down suspicion here on the campus," he advanced, to no one in particular. Then directly to Madge: "It'll be understood that you've been excused to go home, on business, for a few days. An' you," he indicated Ellen, "Miss Vance, can be excused to visit her two or three times a week. You can go back and forth with Doctor Swanson on his visits. Now, young women," he continued cautiously, "this thing must be kept a secret! If it gets out, the reputation of this school will be ruined," He shook his head vigorously. "You've done an awful thing, Miss Conley!" he accused.

This last from him brought resentful tears to Madge's eyes.

"I realize I was foolish to go out with Gill," she admitted, "but does that make his crime against me any the less?"

"Oh, you couldn't prove nothin' 'gainst Mr. Gill!" John's defended his superior. "He's a white man, an' yo' word 'gainst his wouldn't mean a thing down here! You're 'bout to do th' best thing: have this operation and let this thing blow over!"

Madge sat wordless and flushed. She did not, in the least, doubt the truth of his opinion as to what her word would mean against that of the white man. Something within her kept saying, "You brought this trouble upon yourself, now clench your teeth and bear it!" Presently, as out of a restless dream, she said:

"All right, I'm ready to go through with everything! I realize that my life's at stake, but ——"

"Your life isn't in so much danger, Miss Conley," Doctor Swanson put in. "You're in excellent physical condition to survive this operation. Don't worry one bit, you can well trust your life to me," he added encouragingly.

Madge drew a long weary breath.

"I must!" she said, low and with finality.

*   *   *

The fifty mile trip to the city of Braxton was made in silence by the two young woman and Doctor Swanson, in his car. In Braxton, the car turned into the leading Negro residential district. At length, it slowed down and turned into the shady driveway of the Benson Private Sanitarium. The small stucco building was laden with vines and sat far back on a well-trimmed lawn that was thickly dotted with trees and shrubbery. Despite herself Madge was repulsed by the secluded appearance of the place, and felt slightly faint, as she and Ellen followed Doctor Swanson into the modernly equipped waiting room.

Doctor Anthony Benson, tall and of a dark walnut color, met them affably. Afterward, he and Doctor Swanson retired to a private office, leaving Madge thankful to be alone with Ellen once more.

Ellen tried to appear unworried though her heart fairly ached for her unfortunate friend.

Presently, Madge looked at her intently and tried to smile.

"I'm going to be brave!" she promised softly.

"Of course you're going to be brave," Ellen told her encouragingly.

The other's lips quivered slightly and she involuntarily swallowed a lump in her throat.

"Ellen," she said, her voice suddenly husky, "if this operation fails, and I go, you — — you'll never let the facts of my condition reach Mother, will you, Ellen?"

Ellen shook her head:

"No, no!" she said. "Your mother will never know. She'll believe what they tell her — — that it was something else."

Presently, the door of the private room opened and Doctor Swanson came out and stood before them.

"Miss Conley," he said to Madge, "it will be necessary for you to take a treatment of medicine, preliminary to the operation. This will likely require a couple of days. During that time,, Doctor Benson will wait on you. He and your nurse, Miss Bell, will be in shortly and direct you to your ward." With this, Doctor Swanson stepped back into the private room.

Madge turned to Ellen with: "I suppose that mean's that you can return to Avon with Doctor Swanson, dear."

Ellen shook her head reassuringly:

"Not if you wish me to stay, darling," she replied.

"I don't wish to impose on you — — tire you out," Madge said. 'Perhaps it would be better for you to go

now and return with Doctor Swanson when he comes
back to perform the operation — —" she paused suddenly, noting the flush in the other's face, then, "Oh,
Ellen, you're trying to look gloomy!" She smiled a little
courageously and continued, more seriously: "I'm trying
to hope and believe that I'll come through all right, but
in case I don't, I wan't you to remember always that,
next to my mother, I love you above everyone else in the
world, Ellen." Suddenly, she bit her lips.

"I — — I'll remember, Madge," Ellen promised
falteringly. "I love you so much, darling!" she said,
blinking through her tears.

Presently, the two physicians entered the room, followed by Miss Bell, the nurse. Miss Bell was middle-
aged and of dark brown skin. She was portly and her
countenance kindly.

"Miss Conley," Doctor Benson said to Madge, "you
may come with us to your ward now."

The two young women arose and embraced each
other.

"So-long, dear," Madge said. "Don't worry about me.
I know I'll make it all right."

"Of course you'll make it all right, darling!" Ellen
said chokingly.

Quickly Madge turned from her and hastened down
the hall between Doctor Benson and Miss Bell.

Doctor Swanson came foward to Ellen and escorted
her outside to his car.

Beside him, Ellen relaxed in the soft upholstery, as
the car slid smoothly out of the driveway of the **Benson**
Sanitarium. Little in the way of conversation passed between them as the car sped along the pike bound for
Avon Colege. "She's athletic and strong!" Ellen tried
to convince herself of Madge.

*   *   *

Two days later, after many sleepless nights, Ellen
returned to Braxton with Doctor Swanson. Again she

sat in the waiting room of the Benson Sanitarium —
this time alone—awaiting the advent of the hour for
callers.   Her mind wandered aimlessly.   She recalled
Madge as she last saw that pathetic girl—pale and sad-
eyed, silently apprehensive, despite the courageous
"front" she had tried to assume.   Ellen thought she had
never before seen the girl so resigned to a thing—so
stoic in the face of tragedy.   Now that the day was here
for the operation, she prayed that Madge would survive
it.

Presently, the silence in the room in which she sat
waiting was broken by a soft, melodious trill which
came from the corner by a large window.   Ellen looked
in that direction and, for the first time, saw a canary in
a swinging cage.   To her, it seemed ironical that in this
place of suffering and uncertainty lived the tiny har-
binger of cheer.   She moved over to the cage and was
petting the little songster when Miss Bell, the nurse,
entered the room.   She smiled and nodded to Ellen.

"How is she?" Ellen whispered to the nurse.

"Why, she's just doing fine," Miss Bell obliged.   "I've
never before seen one hold up so well under an operation
of this sort," she added.

Ellen gasped at this from her.

"Why, you don't mean to say that the operation has
been performed already?" she said uneasily.

Miss Bell nodded.

"Yes.   Yesterday afternoon," she answered casually.

Ellen faltered, "But, I —— I thought Doctor Swanson was to perform the operation!"

Miss Bell shook her head.

"No, dear," she said, "Doctor Benson always handles
such cases.   "Now," she went on, anxious to avoid more
on the subject, " you may see Miss Conley.   You'll have
about twenty minutes with her."

Gently, the nurse ushered the perplexed girl out of
the room and down the hall to the stairway which they

ascended. Madge occupied a corner ward on the second floor.

Ellen shuddered slightly as Miss Bell cautiously opened the door. The room, laden with the smell of drugs, was spotlessly clean and white, and Madge lay before them on an immaculate bed, the eyes in her pallid face closed.

Moving closer, Ellen gasped at the change misery had wrought on the girl's countenance, and withdrew slightly and involuntarily. Madge's once cherry bow-shaped lips were purple and slightly distorted. Her once glowing cheeks were bloodless and of the deathly color of wax.

"Speak to her," the nurse whispered to her.

Ellen bent over the still figure on the bed and spoke softly:

"Madge!" she said, "it's Ellen, Madge,"

Slowly, as if by supreme effort, the bed-ridden girl opened her dark eye lids and silently regarded Ellen.

As she looked into the afflicted girl's eyes and sensed the terrible pain that they reflected, Ellen felt that she herself would not be able to hold up much longer.

"Darling," she said, softly and brokenly, "don't you know me?"

Slowly, a faint smile formed on the sick girl's face and Ellen beheld recognition in her large, dim eyes. Ever so slightly, Madge nodded her tousled head, then closed her eyes again.

Ellen could not speak to her again; just stood helplessly looking down upon the once dynamic and carefree girl, now so very limp and utterly helpless. Presently, Ellen was conscious of the steadying hand of the nurse on her arm. Turning, she slowly followed the elderly white-clad woman out of the room. Back in the dim hall, she gave way to the tears that had swirled about her heart.

"Poor Madge!" she said to the nurse, chokingly, "it's terrible to see her in this condition. She must have suffered horribly!"

"She hasn't fully recovered from the anesthetic," the nurse said by way of explanation. "She'll come around all right, so don't you worry," she added.

Doctor Swanson awaited Ellen in the reception room. He was ready to return to Avon College. She followed him out to his car and he helped her into the front seat beside him.

"I think Miss Conley is doing fine," he commented as he nosed the car out of the Benson Sanitarium drive.

Ellen sighed wearily before she answered him.

"I hope so," she said.

The pike before them wended its way through the country like a skein of satin ribbon.

Finally Ellen gathered sufficient strength to say:

"Doctor Swanson, I'm surprised that you didn't perform the operation yourself, as you promised her you would."

The doctor was suddenly embarrassed.

"Well," he hedged, "I — — I made her the promise under severe stress. The situation was so very urgent that I didn't realize what I was promising. You see," he went on, thoughtfully, "such an operation is illegal, and as head of Avon College Hospital, I have too much at stake. Doctor Benson is a skilled obstetrician and Miss Conley couldn't be in better hands."

"I see," Ellen replied absently, her mind suspended between what he had said, and the realization, for the first time, that she was a party to an illegal act. But the thought that perhaps Madge's greatest danger was about over, was strangely comforting to her pained conscience. She said no more to Doctor Swanson; just rode the remainder of the way to Avon College in silence.

CHAPTER TWENTY-ONE

Death spared Madge. To her, those two or three weeks of suffering had been nothing more than a mean-

ingless blank in her life out of which she had emerged
with her once strong, athletic body weak and drained of
much of the stamina and zest it once possessed. To
Ellen, those weeks had been an aeon of hope against
fear, leaving her nervous and weak from the strain.

Now it was autumn, and the regular session of college
had begun. Madge was not, by any means, recovered
from her ordeal. Not the least trace of the old, vibrant
flush had returned to her cheeks. In its stead was a
pallor like that of a waxen mask. Her figure was reduced from a harmony of rounded curves to frail, gaunt
lines. Strangely enough, her former dynamic spirit was
gone leaving in its place an uneasy sulkiness—a brooding
stoicism, which expressed itself in her almost constant
silence.

"Ellen," she said, one evening, "have you noticed that
my health isn't improving?"

Ellen had noticed it all right, but she was reluctant
to admit it.

"Well, no — — not exactly — —" she hedged.
"You're quite frail yet, but — —"

Madge shook her head.

"I'm not doing any good!" she interrupted ironically.
"This repeated treatment at the hospital isn't helping me
a bit. I weighed this morning, and I'm still losing. I'm
becoming uneasy about the cold sweats I'm having at
night. I just wonder if — — if — —"

"Well, what does Doctor Swanson say?" Ellen said
quickly.

The other was suddenly still and her eyes dropped to
the floor.

"He insists that it's a deep-seated cold," she said
finally, "but, I know better. You see, I haven't had physical education for nothing. This constant pain between
my shoulders, this stubborn cough, this everlasting weariness — — it's my lungs, Ellen!"

During a brief interval, the other was silent; just
looked into Madge's large, tragic eyes and wished from

the depth of her heart that she could help her. At last, she said:

"Maybe you're just imagining things, Madge." But a slight shudder trailed her words, for, intuitively, she was conscious of the correctness of her friend's diagnosis.

Madge shook her head:

"No!" she said with conviction. "I've a feeling that I'll never be well again!" She smiled, a faint, ironic smile. "It's the 'bugs', Ellen!" she added thickly.

Ellen flushed, "Madge," she began, "I've seen you snap out of many things. It's simply not like you to brood over anything, yet, that's exactly what you're doing now."

Madge shrugged despairingly.

"Who wouldn't brood, in my condition?" she said impatiently. "Wasting away, ounce by ounce! Why, I scarcely have the energy to hope." Her gaze returned to the floor, and, for a moment, she was silent. Then, "well, Mother's after me to come home, and I think I'd better go —— right away! I certainly don't want to die here."

Ellen thought of how lonely she would be here without Madge, but quickly she reasoned that home was the place for one in Madge's condition.

"Doubtless," she said presently, "a change of climate and environment will help you, but I think your fatalism is uncalled for, darling. I'm going to miss you, all right," she added with a sigh.

Madge looked at her, thoughtfully:

"It's going to be hard parting from you, Ellen," she said whimsically "but I guess it's inevitable. Mother'll probably decide to sent me out West," she went on, "but I've got a feeling that it'll do no good to send me anywhere." Presently, she arose, her once snugfitting pajamas now hanging in folds about her frail body, and threw back the cover on her bed.

"Going West," Ellen encouraged soothingly, "has

cured thousands, and it'll cure you, Madge, if you'll just keep up your courage."

Feebly, Madge crawled into her bed.

"I hope so," she whispered between laborious breaths. "Well," she added, "I'm saying goodnight. I need all the sleep I can get."

"Goodnight, darling," Ellen murmured.

Later, in bed herself, Ellen lay thinking of Madge. It seemed so unreal—this change in the girl! Of course, tuberculosis is quite enough to change anyone, she thought.

CHAPTER TWENTY-TWO

A sadly contemplated Sunday afternoon came quickly, perhaps because it held another trying ordeal for the two young teachers—the ordeal of parting, maybe forever.

While she awaited a taxicab to hurry her across the prairie to the tiny shed that was the railroad station at Avon College, Madge tried to be cheerful. A faint smile appeared on her face:

"Ellen," she said, "I was just thinking how you've spoiled me. I guess I'm going to find it awfully hard getting well without you near me. But, I'm — —" she hushed suddenly, her mind submerged in desperate thought. Yes, she was thinking, of course I'm going to fight for my life! Meeting Ellen again will be worth it! Suddenly, tears filled her eyes and trickled down her cheeks.

Ellen, a lump suddenly choking her, came foward and placed an unsteady but soothing arm about the ailing girl:

"Now, darling," she said with emotion, "we mustn't part this way! We must part happily! It's simply that you're going away to get well, and you're going to get well — — if you try. Then, we'll meet again, and laugh and talk about the things that've happened to us here.

Maybe we're going to realize, Madge, that they weren't so bad after all—I mean, in comparison with the experience the outside world probably holds for us."

The honk of the taxicab, opposite their window, did not immediately end their conversation. Madge, in silence, had carefully weighed Ellen's words. Presently, by a supreme effort, she collected every fragment of her shattered courage:

"You're right, Ellen!" she said with finality. "We're going to part happily, just like we met — — and, and I'm going to get well, too!" With this, she arose and picked up her wrap. "The cab is blowing for me. I must be going now."

Ellen arose and handed the girl's traveling bag to the taxi-driver who had just knocked at the door. As he hastened down the hall with it, she returned to Madge who had gotten into her wrap, and gripped her hand:

"I'm not saying goodby, Madge," she said to the pale girl. "It's only so-long 'til we meet again. I'll be writing you the news from here, and I'll want to be hearing from you regularly — —"

"All right, darling," said the other, scarcely above a whisper. "And regardless of what happens to me, you'll do all you can to keep Mother from learning of my —" she paused with an effort at smiling "— my escapade, I guess you'd call it —?"

Ellen nodded. "I promise," she said simply, then turned from the other quickly, avoiding an embrace which she knew would end with a deluge of tears. Somewhere in her consciousness she heard the echo of Madge's "so-long, Ellen," as that sick girl hurried down the hall and out of her life.

Through the window, she could have watched the cab depart with her loved one, but she could not bear to see this, so, she sat down on the side of her bed and looked about the room. Somehow, it already seemed strangely empty and forbidding. She looked at the bed opposite her, which was now so forlornly void of Madge and the coverings so akin to Madge, and wondered how soon this loneliness would force her to give up her position and leave Avon College herself.

*   *   *

To Ellen, the weeks that followed seemed vast stretches of void and loneliness. Madge, with her mother, was now in sunny Arizona, fighting a losing battle for her health. The utter futility of it all was expressed in her gloomy letters. In a recent one, she had described herself as being "only skin and bones," She had said, further:

"I am bedfast, but as long as I can lift a pen, I'm writing you, Ellen. One of these weeks you won't receive a letter from me, then you may know that I've struggled through my last breath, or will be nearing it. When it comes, I shall welcome it. I'm tired, Ellen— tired of this suffering! My nurse is very confidential, and when I am unable to write, she will write you for me, at my dictation. They haven't told me, but their actions prove that all hope for my recovery is gone. The grief and uneasiness in Mother's eyes are proof enough."

Ellen's replies to the sick girl had been full of cheer and encouragement, but she expected to receive word of her death any day, and had so resigned herself.

Today, her classwork had been unusually heavy, and she welcomed the darkness which slowly enveloped the world. She relaxed in the comfort of her small rocker and frowned, suddenly, as she recalled that she had intended to grade papers, but had come away from the conservatory forgetting them. Often she had forgotten important things at the conservatory, and always, she hated the ordeal of having to return to that dark, empty building for them. At last, with reluctance, she threw on her wrap and started for the conservatory. It occupied a five-room cottage which had formerly been used as a family dwelling. A front porch extended across its full width.

As usual, she found the place dismally dark. At the door, she fumbled for her keys while fuming at herself for failing to stop and pick out the right key while passing a campus light in the distance. She did not have to use a key, for presently, a man opened the door from the inside, and hurried past her in the darkness. For a moment, she was frozen with fear. She wondered what man had business in the conservatory at this hour of the night, and how had he gotten in. She managed to remain silent and watch the shadowy hulk until it reached the nearest campus light, then she saw, to her amazement, that it was a white man. Suddenly, she recognized him:

"Gill!" she told herself, low and breathless.

Her puzzlement was overwhelming and she turned again to the door and shoved it open. She felt thankful that the light switch was at the door. As quick as her fingers found it, she snapped on the light. The sight within the room which met her eyes, dazed her for an interval. It was Mrs. Carmelita Johns, the matronly, though good-looking wife of Principal Obadiah Johns. At this moment, Ellen was on more intimate terms with the haughty Carmelita Johns than ever before. Mrs. Johns was really an unusually pretty brown-skinned woman. Now, she stood before her intruder flushed and disheveled, strands of dark, wavy hair loose in her face, as if she had just emerged from a scuffle with some one. Evidently, she had intended to push past Ellen in the dark, but the sudden light had halted her, and now, as if outwitted, she stood with an expression of derision on her flushed face, staring at the younger woman.

"Well?" Mrs. Johns snapped finally.

"Oh, I beg your pardon!" Ellen said breathlessly. "I — — I — —" her effort to explain was cut short by Carmelita Johns who brushed past her, snapped out the light and vanished into the darkness outside.

Dizzily, Ellen searched for the switch then snapped on

the light again. She did not attempt to see more of Mrs. Johns. She felt that she had already seen too much of that woman. Presently, she found the papers that she had intended to grade, on a piano in the room.

As she hurried back to her room, she felt as though she had just emerged from a nightmare into which she had wandered aimlessly. Again in her room, she threw her wrap on the bed and sank down into the rocker. Feebly, her mind was trying to grasp the significance of the situation out of which she had just emerged.

"Carmelita Johns—the Principal's wife!" she muttered, crazily, to herself, "trysting with Gill, a white man!" She clenched her teeth to avoid further utterances, but her thoughts went on wildly: So, even the wife of the Principal is lending herself to the shameful corruption of this place, and with the same white official who had figured in Madge's misfortune! The same white man whose intimate pal was that younger white man who, without doubt, had been involved in Dean Warren's murder, because she dared to interfere with his amorous interest in a Negro girl!

"And yet they boast that the so-called better elements in both races don't mix down here!" Ellen said to herself disgustedly.

Suddenly, a knock at her door snatched her out of her reverie. She opened it, and to her surprise, Mrs. Obadiah Johns faced her. When she had regained herself sufficiently, she invited the woman in.

"Won't you sit down?" she said to Mrs. Johns, indicating a chair.

Mrs. Johns cooly ignored this.

"I came by to speak to you about what you saw tonight," she said.

"Why, I —— I'm not demanding an explanation," Ellen stammered.

"Of course not!" Carmelita Johns said. "You wouldn't dare to!" she added, her pearly teeth glittering through a disdainful grin. "The fact that, perhaps, you wish to keep your position here is why I've come. What you saw tonight would cause unnecessary scandal, if you should tell it. Since I would be involved, it would cost you your position. If you want your position, you — —"

"I don't particularly wish to retain this position!" Ellen interrupted her hotly, "especially since I find that the Principal's wife is contributing to the corruption of this place!" she added with growing anger at the woman's insulting slurs.

This stab from Ellen, with its tone of independence, cooled Carmelita Johns considerably, and her next words were more softly patronizing:

"Well," she said, "I admit that my position with Mr. Gill appeared compromising, but I — — I was more a victim of peculiar circumstances; therefore, I'm begging you not to mention the affair."

"I think I'm quite capable of forming my own opinion about your affair!" Ellen retorted, then shook her head, "Of course, I shan't mention it! I can't afford to so lower myself!" She experienced fiendish satisfaction in seeing the haughty Carmelita Johns so humbled.

"All right," Mrs. Johns said at length, "I shall be grateful to you for the favor." With this, she moved to the door and staggered out, closing it behind her.

Thoroughly disgusted and fatigued, Ellen turned from the door and sat down on her bed. She cupped her chin in her hands and attempted an appraisal of the present situation at Avon College. So far as she herself was concerned, she felt that, tonight, a climax had been reached. Under cover, the place was rotten with scandal and intrigue. Everybody here seemed to be in possession of some secret which he or she was coerced into keeping, by threat of bodily harm or loss of position. Now, she herself was again the unwilling possessor of another secret—the shielder of another wrong, and she was sick of it all!

Presently, she reached a decision which sent her to her

feet. She sat down at the table and addressed a letter
to Madge:

"Dear Madge." she wrote, "I'm hoping that this
will find you better. I write this simply because I'm
full and must confide in someone who knows the situation here. I witnessed something unbelievable, tonight, and it has definitely changed my viewpoint. But,
I shan't defile the mails with a story of what I saw,
and you might not understand anyway. Suffice it to
say that I am thoroughly sick of this place.

"I am convinced that perhaps this 'greater need' to
which Dean Marleigh referred, is not so true of these
students as of those with whom their welfare is in-
trusted; those who are supposed to minister to them.
If it is true that other Southern Negro colleges are
similar to this one, the educational outlook for our
people in the South is certainly gloomy. Perhaps
there's no remedy for the situation so long as these
Negroes must kowtow to the whites for the fragments
they receive for the upkeep of their schools. That
means that this situation shall probably exist always.
Therefore, I'm giving it up—I'm going to Mom and
Mae — —"

But Ellen did not finish writing the letter. Instead,
she laid the pen aside, gathered up the sheets and tore
them to bits. She had suddenly decided that she must
not torture Madge with more disgusting news from this
place. Too, she thought, it might be cowardly for her
to leave this place, which, in spite of everything, yet
needed her services so much, To leave would admit
failure, she thought reproachfully.

But this recent episode in which the Principal's wife
had played so prominent and disgraceful a part, preyed
upon Ellen's mind; shook her morale, more than had any
previous happening, and in a fit of despondency   she
conjured up some sort of an excuse for demanding a
short leave of absence, rather than an acceptance of her
resignation.

"My sister, Mae, is seriously ill," she lied to Principal Johns, next day.

After feigned serious consideration, the Principal granted her a short leave of absence.

She stumbled away from his office sorely exasperated and pricked by her conscience.

"Oh, what this place has done to me!" she cried to herself in amazement. "—A cringing liar, that's what it's made of me!" she added.

But, she decided, stubbornly, that she'd go through with her scheme now, regardless. Maybe a brief change of scene would give her a new perspective of Avon College; give her a breathing spell sufficient to enable her to return to the circle of life there and completely floor the opposing forces that had so shaken her determination to succeed.

She sat down and scribbled a pleasant note to the ill and far-away Madge, telling her of her leave of absence, and informing her to address her at home until further notice.

CHAPTER TWENTY-THREE

On the evening of her departure from Avon College, Ellen's telegram went foward to Mom. Now that Mom had, by way of undaunted courage and dogged persistence, attained such a richly rewarded success in the career which she had chosen to follow, and Ellen, herself, stood on the brink of failure in the career for which she had been so carefully groomed, she felt that their meeting would be touched with irony—an irony of which only she of the three would be conscious, for only she herself was aware of the menacing proximity of her defeat.

On the following day, the train which sped her homeward, crossed the Mason-Dixon Line, and Ellen left the stuffy jim-crow coach for a more comfortable chair-coach. Almost immediately, her cramped feeling left her, Not until then did she fully realize that she was again in an atmosphere which offered greater liberties for people of her beloved Negro race. Now that her money could command the same accomodations as those in the command of the money of members of other racial groups, she stopped the conductor and engaged a pullman berth for tonight and the remainder of her journey home. She wished to present her best appearance when she should step off the train, into Mom's arms, the following morning.

Stealthily, the dark blanket of night settled over the tumbling landscape, and, at an early hour, Ellen relaxed, gratefully, in a lower berth of a dimly lighted pullman. The monotonous click-clack of the rails beneath the hurtling coach lulled her into a drowsy reflection— a reflection which caused her to consider just what could be the deeper meaning of her impulsive and abrupt departure from Avon College, even though it be merely a short leave of absence. She wondered, with sinking heart, if the meaning of it all was not deeply rooted in a form of cowardice of which she was guilty—a yellow streak at whose urge she was sulking away, in utter defeat, from the grim reality of a worthy task which she had, months before, gone forth to accomplish. Had she really failed? She shuddered at the very thought.

Next morning, she got up, feeling refreshed but in no way happy. She dressed daintily and hurried to the dining-coach where she sat down at a table and sipped orange juice, then a cup of black coffee.

Two hours later, she walked out of the train into the union station at home. Somehow, the caress of the chilly air against her cheeks filled her with a bit of the old zest which she had previously enjoyed here in her home-town. A red cap seized her bags and she followed him up the long flight of stairs to the main floor of the station. She was certain that Mom and Mae awaited her, in the crowd up there, and such contemplation made the stairs seem endless to her.

At last, she reached the landing and elbowed her way into the milling crowd, her eyes searching for sight of her loved ones. Presently in her anxious search, she thought of her mother's new interests—a rapidly expanding manufacturing business with, perhaps, a million dollar future!

"Maybe," she said to herself. "maybe they were too busy — —"

Two arms suddenly thrown about her cut her short:

"Darling!" Mom was crying to her.

"Mom!" Ellen cried breathlessly, then, suddenly she was, once again, a sobbing infant in the tender and adoring embrace of her mother.

"Ellen!" It was Mae, pretty and delectable in her emotion.

Coming out of Mom's embrace, Ellen gathered Mae into her arms.

"Mae, darling!" she cried, then kissed the girl again and again.

Their embraces over, Mom regarded Ellen up and down:

"Oh, my dear," she said, "you're looking thin and—and a little older!"

Ellen sighed, ever so slightly.

"I'm not surprised that I do, Mom," she said, "for I feel much older. You know, I've experienced a plenty since I saw you last." She smiled mirthlessly.

"And that poor girl—how did she ever get, Ellen?" Mae wanted to know.

"Oh, Madge, you mean," Ellen suggested, a dart of sadness piercing her heart. "Why, she — — she's worse, darling."

By this time, the three had reached the ornate station plaza out front' and Mom directed the red-cap carrying Ellen's bags, to her car which stood at the curb in all its nickled splendor, brilliant and low-slung. During the time it took the three of them to get into the front seat, with Mae at the wheel, Ellen was speechless with surprise. Presently, her utterance returned to her:

"Mom, you've actually bought a car!" she cried with glee.

Mom merely chuckled and nodded her head.

"Why, it's marvelous!" Ellen exulted, then, "how — really, Mom, has your business reached this stage?"

Mom smiled broadly.

"Honey," she said, "haven't you been reading the colored newspapers?"

"No — — no, I haven't Mom. You see, down there — —" Ellen broke off suddenly, overwhelmed with the admission of success which was expressed in the tone of Mom's question. Then it was all suddenly amusing to her, and she laughed.

"Mom, you cunning old darling!" she cried.

The car was now purring contentedly along Maple Drive, and for the first time, Ellen noticed the unfamiliar (to her) direction in which they were going.

"Is home in this direction?" she asked, her question meant for either one of the other two.

Mae nodded. "About half a mile farther this way," she said.

Ellen turned to Mom in thrilled askance:

"Mom what have you done?" she said happily.

They were now turning into the winding drive of a large, white stone mansion which Mom and Mae had already occupied for several months.

Mom smiled sweetly.

"You must realize," she reminded Ellen, " that your old Mom's in big business, and that requires more pretentious living quarters, servants and the like."

Ellen was aghast at the magnificence of the new place, as Mom and Mae showed her about what was easily one of the most beautiful estates in that section of the city. It seemed to her unbelievable that her mother, or any one else, could have accomplished so much in so short a time.

Once she exclaimed:

"Mom, how did you do it all?"

Mom shook her head:

"I hardly know, myself, darling," she answered. "The work of our good Lord isn't always easy to explain."

*   *   *

Restful and contented like the flow of a woodland brook, were the several days that followed in Ellen's brief recess from a hectic life in the South. It was in the gray of an evening twilight when she came into the library with Mae and found a letter from Madge awaiting her. They were alone in the spacious house. Even Mom's housekeeper was gone.

Ellen picked the letter up and sat down on a divan before the open fireplace to read it. Mae came and sat beside her. Before she opened the letter, Ellen noted that it was addressed in a handwriting which was unfamiliar to her. Presently, she shuddered as she realized what this meant—poor Madge must be nearing death! She was suddenly fearful of facing the letter's contents alone.

"It's from Madge," she told Mae, softly, " let me read it aloud."

"Go ahead," Mae prompted wonderingly.

In a tense voice, Ellen began reading aloud the letter, which said:

"Ellen, my darling Friend: This may be my last letter, as I expect every minute to be my last. Below my window is a bed of beautiful white lilies, Somehow, they hold a strange fascination for me. I guess it's because they remind me of you, Ellen—so pure, clean and undefiled; like I might have been, but for my foolishness. Here I sit, propped in my bed, wishing that I, too, could be like them, so that I might add something worthwhile to the good that's in the world. But, I suppose it's too late.

"Often, I recall that phrase that you were always

repeating at Avon College: 'there's a greater need below'. As I watch these tender lillies, I'm unreasonable enough to wonder if, perhaps, there is now 'a greater need below' the sod for what is left of my wasted body. Maybe there is enough left of me to add some beneficial element to the soil which produces such beautiful flowers. I certainly pray that there is. If so, maybe by this time next spring, I too shall be contributing to the beauty in the world.

"Ellen, my beloved friend, I feel that the hour of my departure is very near, and I want you to know that when it comes, I shall go bravely and thankful for the worthy example which you set for me, even though I failed to follow it.

Lovingly, throughout eternity,
"Madge."

From the changed expression on her older sister's face, Mae realized the deep grief that the pathetic lines of the letter poured into her heart. She saw her bite her lip with restrained emotion when she had finished reading the last line, and wished that she herself could say something to comfort her.

A sharp ring of the doorbell suddenly aroused them from their gloomy silence. Mae arose and hurried toward the door in the front vestibule from which the sound had come.

Ellen heard a man shout "Western Union!" and, for the moment, Madge was the only one that she could associate with a telegram. Involuntarily, she was upon her feet, hastening to Mae's side at the door. She reached the door just as the messenger called her name. Intuitively, she knew that the telegram was from some relative of Madge's—knew that Madge had passed on. She took the telegram, but was too nervous to sign for it.

"Please sign for me, dear," she said to Mae slightly above a whisper. "It's about Madge," she added breathlessly, "Madge is dead! Somehow, I just know it!"

Mae signed for her, then took the telegram which her sister gently pressed into her hand. Her own eyes misty and wide in wonderment, Mae opened it and, in a glance read its terse message of sadness. Quickly, her hand went to Ellen's arm to support her, then the younger girl nodded gravely:

"Yes," she said softly, "Madge is dead!"

She felt Ellen flinch slightly at her words, then quietly escorted the grief-stricken young woman back to the divan.

Again seated upon the divan, Ellen was mutely silent in the grip of that strange aweness which follows in the wake of the death of a loved one. Mae, heroic throughout the tragic interval, sat beside her, gazing intently at the glowing coals in the fireplace. Presently, she said to her sister:

"Would you care to lie down, dear?"

"No, Mae," Ellen answered brokenly, "I only wish to be quiet for a moment. Perhaps I can think a prayer for poor Madge." With this, she rested her head against her little sister's shoulder and closed her eyes in silence.

Mae sat still and collected, and, presently through the corner of an eye, saw her sister's lips move as if in silent prayer. Not wishing to disturb her sister's sacred reverie, she returned her gaze to the flicker in the fireplace. As she sat thus engaged, she felt something warm strike her hand, repeatedly. Presently, she knew that those warm touches were Ellen's tears. Then her arms encircled her older sister's body and drew it close to her own, and she pressed tender lips against the other's bloodless cheeks:

"There now, darling," she said tenderly, "you must get hold of yourself. I'll take her place with you — — I'll be your pal."

This from her little sister brought Ellen's mind back to earth, with the realization that life yet held more to live for than she had lost in the death of Madge—for here, close to her, was her darling younger sister, herself

the embodiment of all the virtue and beauty and sweetness to which Madge's last letter had so pathetically and
yearningly referred.   Too, there was Mom to live for—
loveable, ambitious, God-fearing Mom!

CHAPTER TWENTY-FOUR

Back at Avon College, from her leave of absence
which had ended so sadly with the news of her beloved
friend, Madge's death, Ellen discovered that she had returned to a miniature world that now seemed lonelier
and emptier than ever before.   She thought it strange
that Madge Conley, now that that once vibrant and carefree girl was beyond the grave, lingered in her mind so
persistently.   So long as she had known that Madge was
alive, even though grave illness and many miles separated
them, her loneliness had not seemed so keen and all-
engrossing.   But now, since her pal's death — —

Death! Ellen marveled to herself incredulously, surely
death did not represent the end of things, as she had once
believed, for, in her own mind, Madge was more alive
now than ever before—at least in her memory.

Stealthily, the days and nights, with their yawning
emptiness, for Ellen, passed swiftly on.   Often she wondered just how and why she stayed on at Avon College,
especially since near-poverty at home was no more.
Letters from Mom and Mae were crammed full of the
story of the continuous advancement of Mom's business,
and the almost fabulous fortune in money which it was
daily pouring in upon them.   But nothing lured her from
her dogged determination to remain at Avon College
until she should be able to leave the place with the conscientious feeling that she had actually succeeded there.

One chilly morning she awoke with the realization
that summer, with its stuffy session of school, had fled,
and autumn, with its beginning of a new, regular session,
had come.   She stepped into her morning pajamas and

brewed a cup of tea that she sipped between munches of tasty wafers.

Done eating, she listened, silently, to the shrill laughter of students in her dormitory; all new arrivals for the autumn session of school. Outside her window, girls were hurrying to and fro on the campus; this and that girl rushing, arm stretched out, to some other girl who had just arrived. She noted that the students were still streaming onto the campus, on foot, automobile and bus.

Presently, on the sidewalk, opposite her window, two shrieking girls hugged each other. She lived again the joy that she knew was in their hearts. It reminded her of her own undergraduate days in which she had faced life with the same youthful, exuberant abandonment with which these girls were now facing it.

A spirited rap on her door snatched her from her reminiscence, and she hurried across the room and opened it in the face of prettey Gail Hines—of all persons, Gail Hines whose escapades both with and without Madge, had precipitated so much trouble on the campus.

Gail deliberately fell into her arms:

"Ellen!" cried the little hoyden breathlessly.

"Gail! darling!" Ellen cried in amazement. "What are you doing back here? I thought you were to complete your college work at —— ——"

"Well, you've another thought coming!" Gail cut her short, laughingly. "Oh," she went on, "I suppose I'm back here to finish breaking up hell! I was careful to flunk out in everything at Tuskegee last year, so's I could have one more year to put in here, you know.: Say" she continued, changing the subject, "I've got to see Madge the very first thing! Where is she?" For the first time, she scanned the room, and her eyes stopped at where Madge's bed had formerly stood. "Oh!" she said with surprise, "you and Madge are not roomng together any more?"

Slowly, Ellen shook her head. "N—No," she stammered, realizing that evidently the girl had not heard of what happened to Madge.

Gail stared at her anxiously:

"Well, where's she staying?" she asked, then she went on, unmindful of the expression of hesitancy on Ellen's face, "you know, I'm opening up the session with a 'heavy date' this very night, and I want Madge to date up her fellow and come along with us." With this, she laughed mischeviously and embraced Ellen again.

"Ellen," she chattered on, not permitting the other a word in edgewise, "I guess you think I'm still the silliest something — — oh! what's the matter, Ellen?" Quickly she released Ellen, stepped back to arm's length and regarded her seriously. Somehow, she had felt the shudder that coursed through Ellen's body.

"Please!" she begged in alarm. "What is it, Ellen? Has Madge gone home?" Quickly the anxious girl scanned the room again, as if searching for some evidence of Madge. Then she turned again to Ellen who had now got control of herself somewhat.

"Darling," Ellen said softly, "and you really haven't heard it?"

"Heard what?" Gail asked with quickened breath. "Oh, my God, Ellen, get me out of this awful suspense! What's happened to Madge?" This last was almost a sob.

Momentarily, Ellen felt as if she'd scream herself, but somehow, she managed to remain calm.

"She's — —she's dead, Gail!" she whispered softly.

"Madge dead? No! No!" Gail screamed.

For an interval, Ellen could not answer. She nodded slowly as tears trickled down her cheeks—tears that evidenced a heart which bled under this ordeal of breaking the news to Gail whom Madge had loved and never grown tired of admiring.

For a moment, Gail stared at her—an expressionless stare—then, struck cold by the note of sincerity in her words, dropped upon the bed with a gesture of futility, and buried her head in a pillow. The girl's sobs, though almost inaudible, were bitter. For the first time in her carefree life, she was feeling the unkind touch of tragedy.

Ellen came and sat down beside her.

"There now, darling," she comforted her, "you must be brave and bear it! Madge wouldn't wish you to grieve for her like this. You must remember, she was always a very brave girl herself. She died bravely — —"

Finally, Gail sat up and listened, silently and intently, to Ellen's story of Madge's tragedy and death.

Her story finished, Ellen asked:

"You loved her dearly, didn't you?"

The girl sighed disconsolately.

"Of course I did," she said softly. "I still love her!" she added as though to herself.

"Well," Ellen went on cautiously, "there's something that I'm certain she'd be glad for you to do in memory of her. I'm wondering if you would be willing to do it?"

Gail's eyes brightened.

"Why — — why, of course I'd do it," she said, puzzled, "I'd do anything I thought Madge would wish me to do for her — —"

Slowly, Ellen nodded approval:

"You know," she said, thoughtfully, "I believe Madge would be very happy, if she could know that you had quit having affairs with this white man, Ellery Perry, and any other white man. What do you think about it? Do you believe as I do?"

The dark lashes that so luxuriantly fringed Gail's large wistful eyes dropped toward the floor, and, for an interval, she sat silent, as if trying to settle, once and for all, a disturbing conflict within her. Presently, as though struck by a new conviction, she nodded:

"I believe as you do, Ellen," she said simply.

"Then — —?" the other paused thoughtfully.

"I'll quit, Ellen!" she promised with finality, then, as if to herself only, "I could never love a white man anyway!"

Ellen's face brightened and she burst, suddenly, into tears of joyfulness:

"Oh, Gail, my darling!" she cried, wringing her hands in ecstacy, "I'm so happy that you've come to yourself!— —" she paused and, then for the moment, studied the other. "At heart, Gail, you're really a good girl!"

CHAPTER TWENTY-FIVE

Now, as ever, little diversion, in the way of social entertainment, was permitted the single faculty members at Avon College. Even though it was a state institution, its normal freedom, if ever it enjoyed any, had long since been over-shadowed by the influence of Principal Obadiah Johns, who had come there from the presidential chair of a small denominational institution in another section of the state; one of the many Southern Negro church-schools that are, even to this modern day, cramped and stagnant under puritanical bigotry handed down from an earlier era. Therefore, only twice a year were the faculty members permitted a dance on the campus of Avon College, and upon those occasions, Principal Johns, feeling himself tolerant to a fault, always stole discreetly away from the campus only to return the next day and dictate letters of dire threat to those single faculty members whose modern gaiety at the dance; such as, perhaps, the indulgence in a forbidden cigarette, had fallen under the sharp, censoring eyes of the fox-like treasurer, Jesse Sales. The end of many an unwary young faculty member's career at Avon College had had its beginning in Jesse Sales' office after a dance.

No wonder, Ellen thought to herself, that it was going to be so hard to forget Madge, for one had little to do but sit in her room, after working hours, and read, if she could, or perhaps nod, until bed time; unless Gail should happen to breeze in with a new repertoire of campus gossip.

But this evening, Ellen had an engagement in the conservatory—one which threatened to be an ordeal, for, over the telephone, that afternoon, she had promised to meet Mrs. Carmelita Johns, the Principal's wife, there. Carmelita had declared that such a meeting between them was very urgent, "for it seriously concerns someone in whose happiness, I understand, you are very much interested," Mrs. Johns said.

Now, having come to the conservatory, Ellen restlessly paced the floor, while outside twilight melted into darkness.

The voice of Carmelita Johns had been soft enough over the telephone, but it had carried an evil tone. Ellen reflected upon her life since that first clash she had had with the venomous woman. Now, for the second time, she must face her again. Now, Carmelita Johns had her frankly puzzled. Who was that "someone" to whom that evil woman referred? There was Gail Hines, Ellen reminded herself—and how much she loved Gail now!—but surely it couldn't be Gail, for a marvelous change had come over Gail since that girl had first learned of Madge's tragedy. Gail had made her a certain promise in memory of Madge, and, thus far, she had kept it religiously.

At last, after what, to Ellen, seemed an eternity, Carmelita Johns came. With anger and hatred gleaming in her malevolent eyes, she deliberately refused the seat Ellen proffered her. Ellen stood, too, facing the matronly woman.

Carmelita opened the skirmish with a question hurled through lips that were twisted in a smirk:

"Is it really true that you're one of those around here who promised Madge Conley that you'd keep the facts of her sickness from her mother?" she wanted to know.

For a moment, Ellen stood before her in speechless dismay. What evil thing did this woman have in mind to do? she wondered. Before she made audible answer she

looked the woman squarely into her serpentine eyes, then
nodded:

"Yes —— —" she answered her simply.

Quickly Carmelita shifted her piercing gaze from her,
then returned it to her, this time with a cruel glow of
triumph in her eyes:

"Well," she said finally, "that isn't exactly what I
came to talk with you about. I happen to know that
there's only one person on this campus—even if all the
rest of them knew about it—that would dare tell about
what you saw that night when you broke in on me in this
conservatory. You are that person, Ellen Vance! The
rumor is out, and you started it!"

For a moment, Ellen was staggered by the woman's
accusations. Her every nerve and fibre rose in rebellion
against Carmelita Johns, but her mind persisted in its
frantic search for reason. Dizzily and hazily, she recalled that night of Carmelita Johns' compromising affair
with that white official, and heard again the retreating
footsteps of those male students who had doubtlessly
seen; first, the white man leaving hurriedly, then Carmelita herself leaving a little later.

"No!" Ellen heard herself denying to Carmelita, "I
never started any rumor on you!"

"You're a dirty lie!" Carmelita blazed, "you were
the only other person that knew anything about it,
and —— —" she paused.

"B—But, you're mistaken," Ellen defended herself.
"I'm sure I heard students retreating outside as you left
the conservatory that night. Has it occured to you that
they might have told it?"

"No!" Carmelita shot. "Only a filthy little wench like
you would dare —— —"

"Don't you call me that again!" Ellen cried furiously,
the while advancing madly upon the other who slunk
backward from her.

Still backing toward the door, Carmelita said:

"Nevertheless, I'm going to get even with you, do you

understand? I'm going to write Madge Conley's mother and tell her the truth about the cause of Madge's death!" She chuckled tauntingly.

For a brief interval, Ellen stood dazed and speechless. Then, piece by piece, her reasoning returned to her, grasping the dire import of the woman's venomous threat. Death! she thought frantically—death, perhaps, to Madge's mother, if she were told the facts of her daughter's tragedy. She advanced no closer upon Carmelita Johns who now stood against the door, facing her, a grin of hate twisting the corners of her heavily carmined lips. Ellen had a sudden impulse to spring upon the woman and tear her to pieces, but, somehow, she restrained herself. Somewhere beneath the hatred that exuded from Carmelita Johns must surely be a tender spot; at least for innocent, trusting mothers, Ellen reasoned, and she herself must, in some way, probe through her base exterior to this spot. Wrath was not the instrument for doing this.

Finally:

"Mrs. Johns," she said pleadingly, "why would you make that poor woman suffer more? Do you realize that the truth about her daughter's misfortune might break her heart — — grieve her to death? Why, to write her such a letter would be a most cruel and cowardly deed—"

"No more cruel and cowardly than this disgraceful lie you've spread on this campus about me!" Carmelita replied hotly.

"But, you're mistaken!" Ellen protested, a lump forming in her throat. "I — — well, I told you, that night, that I wouldn't so lower myself as to — —"

Carmelita cut her short:

"If you were low enough to hide your friend's abortion and murder from her mother, there's nothing else too low for you to do!" With this, Carmelita opened the door, hurried out and slammed it behind her.

Ellen stood speechless, staring blankly at the door. Abortion! Murder! Those words in connection with

Madge's misfortune, stunned her. Abortion and murder were serious crimes, she reasoned. But, was she herself a party to a crime, because, at Madge's dying behest, she had mercifully refrained from writing that girl's mother the facts in the case? Really, there had been no occasion to do so. Evidently, Madge's mother had not questioned the reasons given for her daughter's illness, by the Doctors Swanson and Benson.

Her soul in turmoil, Ellen staggered to the desk in the room and slumped down in the chair before it. What was she to do to head the woman off? Carmelita Johns was a vengeful woman and would doubtless carry out her wicked threat. Fearful suppositions raced through Ellen's clouded mind as she sought a way to prevent Carmelita's avowed purpose.

"I must do something to stop her!" she told herself frantically.

Presently, the door opened and Gail Hines stood before her, framed in it. Quickly Ellen tried to suppress the tears that simply would not be held back. Noting this, Gail's smile changed to an expression of surprise.

"Oh, Ellen!" she cried. "What's the matter?" She hurried to the older girl and faced her across the desk.

"Gail!" Ellen said brokenly, "what am I to do? It's that Johns woman —— she's ——" she paused suddenly, interrupted by Gail:

"The dirty cow!" Gail was saying, "I saw her come out of here, and I just knew she was up to something evil! That's why I came."

"Gail," the other sobbed, "she's going to write Madge's mother the truth about the cause of Madge's death! She's —— oh, but you must help me stop her somehow!"

Gail moved around the desk and laid a comforting hand upon her shoulder:

"There now," she said, "just you get hold of yourself. There must be some way to stop her! let me think." She was suddenly quiet, as if thinking deeply. Then, suddenly, she brightened with a new idea: "Ellen!" she said hastily, "I have it, Ellen! The address of Madge's mother is in only one place on this campus, outside this room —— it's on her application blank in a file in the Principal's office! Carmelita Johns will have to get it there.   Listen, dear," she snapped her fingers triumphantly, "I'll get it out of that file tonight! Johns is in his office every night until late, and he's got a 'crush' on me anyway —— been begging me to visit him up there for a long time.   I'll surprise him tonight, and Carmelita Johns will *not* get to do this dirty thing!"

This from the fiery mulatto girl stunned Ellen.

"No, Gail," she protested thoughtfully, "you must not meet him! I can't let you compromise yourself with him, under any circumstances!"

Gail nodded—a nod which bespoke dogged determination to carry out her plan.

"It's all set!" she declared. "Of course I'll meet him, this very night, and get that application form!"

"But, Gail —— Gail, you ——"

"Just hush right up, Ellen," Gail admonished. "I'll be doing it for Madge!" She started for the door, then, a sudden thought striking her, stopped there, turned and looked back at Ellen who had watched her every move, with an expression of futility and resignation mixed.

"Listen, Ellen," Gail said with finality, "you come to his office at exactly eleven-thirty.   I'll see that the night-latch is left off, and you open the door and walk right in.   You see, force might be necessary to get hold of that application.   Now, you come.   Surely you won't fail poor Madge!"

Slowly, hesitantly, Ellen nodded, then watched the door close behind the little bundle of lightning known as Gail Hines.

CHAPTER TWENTY-SIX

Nervously, dejectedly, Ellen watched the clock in her room. The hands pointed to eleven o'clock. She felt as if the hour of doom for her must be close at hand, for she could not so much as imagine just what steps the fiery Gail Hines intended to take to secure the vital application form on which was the address of the deceased Madge Conley's mother. Gail had said that force might be necessary to get it. Force! What sort of force? Ellen wondered. If Gail had meant physical force, what chance would two frail young women have against a raw-boned giant like Principal Obadiah Johns? Did Gail intend to be prepared to hold him up at the point of a gun? That would be robbery, a serious crime! Ellen was thoroughly frightened.

"No, I shan't go!" she told herself fearfully.

But, Gail's reminder sounded again in her unwilling ears:

"Surely you won't fail poor Madge!"

She shuddered and clenched her teeth:

"No!" she told herself, "I won't fail Madge —— I can't fail her! I —— I'll go, come what may!"

She glanced at the clock. The hands pointed to eleven-twenty-five —— only five more minutes in which to go! she realized.

Qiuckly, almost savagely, she snatched up her wrap, threw it on, and stole quietly out of the room and out of the building. As she hurried across the campus to the darkened administration building, a queer sort of coldness gripped at her heart.

"Yes, I'll go!" she kept saying to herself.

Finally, she reached the little vestibule before the door of Principal Johns' office. For the first time, she realized that the entire campus was dismally quiet—even the dormitories on the men's side. A mere trickle of light sifted through a crack in the lowered blind at the Principal's door.

While Ellen stood there in the dark, trying to muster up sufficient courage to open the door, someone—she immediately recognized it to be Carmelita Johns herself—stepped quickly out of the darkness in a corner of the vestibule and shoved the door open.

The sight within the office, which confronted the two women, stunned them, and for a moment, they stood side by side as if frozen to the spot.

There before them sat Gail on Obadiah John's lap, her head resting languidly against his bald head.

Carmelita was furious:

"So this is the sort of 'business' that keeps you here so awfully late these nights, is it?" she demanded to know of her husband, who was at once all awkward gestures and violent frowns, in his surprise.

During the tense, threatening silence, Gail, a wicked smile on her face, slid off the Principal's lap, snatched the application form from his desk and hurried to the astonished Ellen and the door. Shortly thereafter, the two were hurrying across the campus to their room.

"Well, here it is," Gail said, handing Ellen the form.

Reluctantly, Ellen took the sheet of paper and nervously crumpled it in her hand.

"That's it," Gail said, "tear it up, if you wish—just so that crooked she-viper doesn't get it. I've given her something to meddle with, instead of Madge's mother—a good reason to vent her spleen on her old man!" She stopped suddenly, then, "why the silence, Ellen? Are you still speechless?"

"Oh!" Ellen gasped, coming back to herself, "th—thank you, dear. B—But, I suppose we'll both have to leave this place after all this."

Gail suddenly slowed her pace.

"Well," she began impatiently, "what the hell if we do? At least, we've saved Madge to her poor old mother! Why should you care anyway? You're rich—you don't

particularly need a job! Anyway, Ellen, you're a damned
silly fool for staying here this long!"

"But, Gail," Ellen protested, "I feel it my duty to —
to —"

"Ah, forget it, sister!" Gail snapped, cutting her short.
"I say you're a fool to stay here another minute! What
the hell good can you do here—you or any one else? If
you just must teach—you've got plenty money—why
couldn't you go home and establish a school of your own,
where you'll be free to teach students as you think they
should be taught? You'll never be allowed to do it
here!"

"But, Gail, you don't understand," Ellen explained as
they came to a halt before the door of her darkened
dormitory.

"Of course I understand," the other cut in. "I understand that you're entirely too decent to continue hanging
on in this hell hole!"

"But, they — —" Ellen paused. What had she intended to say?

"They don't mean you a darn' bit of good!" Gail
supplied, then, "listen, Ellen," she went on warningly,
"after what's happened tonight, you and I had better
get away from here as quickly as we can! That Carmelita
Johns—the nasty sow!—will make it hot for us, if we
don't! Oh," she shrugged, "stay if you want to, but I'm
packing tonight, and tomorrow, I'm grabbing on to the
first 'Jim-Crow' coach truckin' my way."

Gail's sudden decision staggered Ellen somewhat:

"But, Gail," she protested, "we can't afford to leave
here so abruptly as that."

"I can," Gail replied cooly, then hastened on, "well,
goodnight dear, I'll be by to tell you goodby later this
morning," She walked away toward her dormitory, heed-
less of Ellen's exasperated "goodnight, Gail."

When she reached her room, Ellen stood before the
haggard image of herself in the mirror of her dressing
table. Presently, she sat down on the bench before it,

with the feeling that something dark and ominous was closing in upon her, threatening to crush her. She wondered frantically what she should do. She had tried so hard to get along and succeed at Avon College. Now, there was that vengeful Carmelita Johns to reckon with! As sure as Gail had said it, Gail was leaving, she thought, while she herself would be left alone to face it all. Could she really afford to leave this place so abruptly, as Gail was leaving it?

Suddenly, she was assailed by the thought:

"Why not? You're free—just like Gail and all the others—to do as you please! You've actually done your best to make it at this place, so why not leave immediately?"

Quickly she reached a decision which was final:

"I shall!" she said aloud to her conscsience. "I'll leave this very afternoon!" she added with finality.

She did not go to bed; instead she spent the remainder of the night packing her trunk and traveling bag.

Shortly after daybreak, Gail came by to tell her goodbye. Gail was quick in taking in the situation:

"So, at last, you've come to your senses!" she commented smilingly.

Ellen breathed deeply and thoughtfully:

"Yes, I suppose I have, Gail," she admitted. "I'm leaving here too."

"What time?" Gail asked casually.

"This afternoon, at three."

"Say," Gail said, "I wish we were going in the same direction, I'd wait for you." A lump rose in her throat suddenly, and she changed the subject: "Ellen, Darling," she said wistfully, "you're as good as gold! I suppose I'll always love and remember you. You've meant so much to me, since Madge — —" she broke off suddenly, unable to finish her reference to Madge lest she burst into sobs.

Ellen tried to smile bravely.

"Gail," she said, "I love you, too; mostly because you

thought enough of Madge to stop playing around so dangerously with white men. I hope you'll never play around that way again. Do you promise?"

Involuntarily, Gail daubed a handkerchief to her smarting eyes, then fished a slip of paper out of her handbag and handed it to Ellen.

"I —— I promise, Ellen," she said. "Please believe me, Ellen," Then she nodded to the slip of paper now in Ellen's hand: "That's my address," she said, "Please write me, Ellen —— often."

The two embraced each other, then Gail turned hurriedly:

"So long, dear," she called back, chokingly, over her shoulder.

With an effort, Ellen blinked away the tears that blinded her.

"Goodbye, Gail," she said softly, the very words clutching at her heart.

For a full minute, she listened, unwillingly, to Gail's receding footsteps down the hall. She felt that, somehow, they tapped out a pathetic farewell which meant forever. Actually, Gail was hurrying out of her life quite as abruptly as that care-free girl had entered it.

Somewhat unsteadily, Ellen returned to her packing. And as she tucked filmy underthings into her bag, she mentally compared Gail with Madge Conley:

"As alike at heart as two peas!" she mused.

Those snappy steps of Gail's—to what end would they lead her? Ellen wondered restlessly.

CHAPTER TWENTY-SEVEN

Fleeting years!

How many years had passed since? Ten—or was it five? No, no! It had been only three years since her final departure from Avon College, Ellen decided.

She got out of bed and looked at the pink-splashed sky

of an early morning, through the tall window of her
boudoir, one of many luxurious rooms in Mom Vance's
much publicized suburban mansion.   Below her lay a
spacious sunken garden awaiting the brilliant rays of the
sun that would transform it into a riot of rich, autumnal
colors.

She breathed deeply and marveled, inwardly, at the
change wealth had wrought upon the three of them—
Mom, Mae and herself.   During these years they had
been the constant talk of the Negro press.   Only if they
would forget us Vances, she complained, at least for a
few years!   Then those newspaper headlines flashed
through her mind again and she saw them as vividly as
if she were holding a copy of the Pittsburgh Courier in
her hands:

Noted Race Benefactress Endows Hospital
Baby Daughter of Toilet Goods Magnate Pledged to
   Sorority
Ellen Vance, Toilet Goods Heiress, Sails for Europe
Madam Anice Vance's Mansion Mecca of Sightseers

What a stride they had made from that tiny flat of
years back!   No wonder that the years had seemed so
many to Ellen!   Millions and millions of people would
never accomplish, in their lifetimes, so much as Mom
Vance had accomplished in hers.   Well, Ellen compro-
mised to herself, Mom's record was really something to
rave about.   And Mom had remained so unruffled and
sweet through it all!   Although Mom detested so much
publicity, she had not complained once—just conceded it
all as the right of the press.

Ellen admitted that she herself was happy, save for
one discordant thought which came often to haunt her:
Where was Dewalt Brooks, that ambitious, impulsive
young man who had so abruptly entered her life enroute
to Avon College years before, and as abruptly walked
out of it?   Could it be that he had not yet accomplished

in life sufficiently to write her letters "filled with sunshine" as he had once promised to do? Was it possible that he had actually lost track of her? Was it that he never read the newspapers, or was he failing to connect her with the wealthy family of Vances so often mentioned in the papers? Maybe he had plainly forgotten her. Maybe he hadn't — —

She did not finish the thought; she did not wish to finish such a miserable thought. Thanks to the door which opened behind her. It was Mom herself coming through the door, a slender slip of paper in her hand. Mom smiled infectiously:

"My lady," she said, "you looked so weary last night that I put this matter off until this morning." She proffered her daughter the slip of paper. "This," she said, "is the check for the first unit of that new sort of school you've been wanting to establish."

Ellen took the check, then gasped at the figures she read on it.

"Mom!" she cried, "why, — — why, it's for a hundred thousand! I — — I hadn't planned to ask you for more than ten or fifteen thousand, then with that as a starter, I intended to make a tour through the country to solicit the remainder of the fund from others. But, now — —"

"You're not going a step to solicit anything," Mom cut her short. "We'll finance that school and enjoy our money while we live."

Ellen felt a tightening in her throat, and before she realized it, was embracing her mother.

"Mom, you darling angel!" she cried.

Mom kissed her—kissed away the tears of ecstasy that tumbled down the girl's flushed cheeks.

"Bless your little heart, honey," Mom said, smiling through misty eyes, "you deserve every cent of it, and more! Didn't you go down into the deep South and work and make all this possible? Of course you did!"

"No, no, Mom dear," Ellen argued, "you're due all

the credit for this—you and your incessant stirring in kettles and tinkering with formulas. Why, Mom, it's all due to your remarkable ingenuity—your —"

Mom raised a cautioning finger to her lips:

"Sh—sh!" she said, "I'll hear to no more of it! Just recall how you cooked and scrubbed your way through the university, then with your hard-earned education—"

"Education!" Ellen broke in, withdrawing from her mother's embrace, "often I've thought, Mom, that from the standpoint of education, I've been a decided failure. We're taught that the purpose of education is to fit men and women for accomplishment in life—for overcoming obstacles sufficiently to reach their aims. In the South, I discovered an even greater need than what I had at first expected to find. I saw what I thought was a chance to really accomplish in life by administering to that greater and more fundamental need, and then — — oh, Mom, you've heard the rest too often — —"

"Of course I have, honey," Mom consoled, "but you're not to blame because you couldn't do anything about it."

"But, maybe I didn't try hard enough, Mom," she suggested thoughtfully, "maybe — — maybe if I had had the courage that you have, I'd be there now fighting and gradually surmounting the difficulties that confronted me, instead of being here doubting and questioning the education I'm supposed to have,"

Mom looked at the girl seriously and questioningly. Presently she said: "Darling lamb, you have got education—a good education—as much education as any girl or boy ever got at Northern University. I'm certain the others are not doubting what they learned there. You've always had plenty of courage, or you wouldn't have gone south in the first place."

Ellen gave her mother a wistful smile, then sighed disconsolately:

"No, Mom," she said, shaking her head slowly, "the moment my degree was handed me was the moment I lost the brand of courage that you have. That moment marked the end of my courage, my initiative; for in it, I subconsciously hoisted that degree between me and the realities of life—as though it alone could win for me— and walked off that rostrum feeling that I had only to make a gesture and the degree would ever after do the rest for me.   Perhaps hundreds of other college trained Negroes of today are going, or have gone, through the same experience.   The older heads of the race may be right in their contention that too many of us emerge from college training without initiative.

"I don't know," Ellen continued thoughtfully, "maybe the fault isn't ours.   Really, Mom, I've begun to wonder if the white man's education which is designed primarily for whites, really fits the Negro to successfully cope with his own problems — —"

"There now, that's enough!" Mom admonished, interrupting her doubtful daughter, "just you — —"

"But you must listen to me, Mom," she protested. "Now, just consider yourself: you never had the privilege of getting formal education. yet, you've accomplished your aim.   You're one of the wealthiest Negroes in the world already, and perhaps you're the race's greatest living philanthropist—all the result of your indomitable courage, common sense, judgment and initiative.

"Why, Mom." she brandished the check she held, "just consider what you're doing this morning—giving me a check for a hundred thousand dollars as unceremoniously as if it were for only one dollar, to finance the revolutionary dream of one who admits failure already.   Who knows but that if you had earned a degree founded upon an education planned primarily for whites and their problems, you would ever have accomplished what you have?   Chances are that, like myself and many others, you might have left it all to the degree alone to accomplish."

Mom's impulse to leave her daughter alone with her pessimistic utterances subsided at this last from her, for it lead the elderly woman into a new line of reasoning.

She was thinking: Perhaps, after all, there was much truth in what the girl had said. Why, even the majority of Negro college graduates of her own generation—what had they done? What were they doing save holding jobs that had already been created for them. Few of them had created anything in the way of business, for these poor young Negroes of today to enter into after finishing school.

Ellen was still talking:

"But, Mom, I'm not giving up. This money of yours is enough to enable me to thoroughly demonstrate this unheard-of idea of mine. I shall establish a new type of school for Negro youth—one whose brand of educational training will prepare them for the more fundamental needs of the race. Maybe, in a few years, you will not have to depend upon whites to plan your factory enlargements; direct your advertising campaigns; handle your problems of production, and advise you on investments. I'll start a search for Dewalt Brooks, a young man I met on my first trip to Avon College, and with this money, we'll revolutionize the Negro race by giving its youth a training fit for its peculiar needs."

By this time, Mom had reached the door:

"Why, of course you've got courage!" she said over her shoulder. "You've simply been disappointed, that's all." Then, Mom laughed gently. "You're still a chip off the old block, honey," she said, a little boastfully, then stepped through the door, closing it behind her.

CHAPTER TWENTY-EIGHT

Dewalt Brooks!

Ellen sat down at the delicately carved spinet desk, fully determined to find him. A little nervously, she withdrew from a tiny drawer the several letters she had received from him many months ago. Before her fingers had untied the purple ribbon about them, her mind wan-

dered dreamily back through the years and recalled all
that had transpired in her life during her hectic period
of trying to administer to the youth of her race.

Through it all, she had grasped futilely at success only
to give it up with the feeling that she had missed it. She
had embraced love only to lose it. She had clung to glorious companionship only for death to step in and ruth-
lessly sever it.

That love, as symbolized by Dewalt Brooks, had suddenly caressed her life and as suddenly vanished from it,
leaving her existence woefully vacant, save for the warm,
intimate companionship of Madge Conley. Then death,
the inexhorable, had player a cruel hand and the impulsive Madge Conley was no more. Try as she had,
Ellen was never able to divorce herself from the conviction that the career upon which she had ventured those
years before had been a miserable failure—despite
Mom's insistence to the contrary. She felt that it had
been thus because she had not been able to depart from
Avon College with the satisfaction that she was leaving
that institution just a little better because of her having
been there.

True that the money she had made while there had
been the foundation of Mom's phenominal success in the
manufacturing business, yet the realization of this was of
little compensation to Ellen, compared with the intan-
gible things she felt that she had lost.

Despite the thousands of dollars that rolled into the
family coffers each month, by way of her mother's sen-
sational "La Mae" toilet products, and the life of ease
and luxury into which their former existence had been
transformed, Ellen realized that after all, things had
seemed terribly vacant and meaningless to her. That
trip to Europe which she and Mae had taken last fall;
that bon voyage party in New York, given them by admiring friends, that handsome stateroom on the great
French ship Normandie, filled to brimming with fragrant
flowers; Mom's proud and smiling farewell benediction;

Mae's sparkling eyes and burbling laughter; the calculating, flattering and flirtatious attentions of that glam-
orous young Ethiopian count (or was it prince?) in Paris,
and their fond farewell to him as he sailed away on a
liner bound for his war-torn homeland to lead an army
of courageous warriors in its defense! Except for the
moment, none of it had meant much to Ellen. That trip
might have been her honeymoon trip with Dewalt
Brooks, if —— ·

Presently, her mind came back to the task at
hand—that of finding Dewalt and proffering him the opportunity of joining her in the thrilling work of trans-
forming into reality their great dream of an institution
based upon a new and revolutionary idea for the practical training of Negro youth. Would he come? she
wondered, or had he lost his great ambition during these
years? Maybe, after all, their affair had not really
mattered to him so much as he had pretended. He might,
after all, be married to another already! Ellen shuddered at the very thoughts.

She directed her letter to the address he had given in
his last letter to her. After it was finished, and she was
slipping it into an envelope, she felt a sudden impulse to
tear it to bits because she imagined that he might, somehow, discern between its very formal business-like lines
the yearning that swelled deep in her heart for him. If
so, she reasoned dismally, he might take it that she was
pridelessly surrendering herself to him—chasing after
him! But she got hold of herself and did not destroy the
letter; instead, she wrote, "Please forward, if not at
this address," upon the face of the envelope.

CHAPTER TWENTY-NINE

Weeks!
To Ellen, they were long, hopeful, anxious weeks that
passed since her letter had been mailed to Dewalt Brooks.

He should have received it by this time, she thought, and if so, surely he at least owed her the courtesy of a reply.

At last, one evening, the reply to her letter came—Dewalt Brooks himself! He told her a story of defeat. The corns and scars on his hands, and the weary, dejected expression in his eyes, were evidence enough of the hardship he had undergone since leaving her at Avon College. Her letter had finally reached him at the scene of a remote Government relief project in a Southern state, on which he had worked months with pick and shovel.

"But, Dewalt, with your knowledge of business procedure and accountancy, you were entitled to better consideration—a 'white collar' position," she argued, the while seeing the expression of futility cloud his face.

He tried to smile and shook his head, a little ironically.

"Not in that state," he declared, then added, a little whimsically, "I'm a Negro, you know. Although I passed every examination I was allowed to take, it made absolutely no difference."

She looked at him intently, a little surprised.

"You — — you mean to say that the Government — the Government —"

He nodded vigorously, cutting her short.

"Yes," he said disgustedly, "the Government—they didn't recognize my qualifications. Down there, on such a project as that, a Negro's qualifications regardless of what they really are, are not considered above that of handling a pick and shovel."

"B—But. the Government — —" Ellen paused, in an effort to realize the significance of his words regarding the unfairness of the Government.

"Oh, the Government! the Government!" he repeated disdainfully, "what this Government means to a Negro depends solely upon what section of the country he happens to be caught in! Anyway, suppose we just drop that subject!" he added angrily.

For an interval, both of them were silent. She knew that anger of the most bitter sort, rankled in his heart.

Presently, what seemed to her the truth of his last words about the Government dawned upon her as she thought of such notorious examples of Government laxity as the defeat of the Dyer Anti-Lynching Bill, the Scottsboro case in Alabama, and other cases of the sort.

Presently, he broke their silence:

"You know," he said, reflectively, "you and your mother have wrought wonders since I saw you last. Now, you challenge me to come and match your accomplishments, and on your own money. May'be I'm a little cowardly and cheap to be accepting your challenge."

Her anxious heart missed a beat. Surely, she thought, this cannot be the Dewalt Brooks of Avon College days talking! His words, and the tone in which he uttered them, seemed the expression of a different man—a man struggling in the throes of wounded pride, or could it be plain jealousy? she wondered.

Finally, she said: "Dewalt, just what do you mean? Surely, you don't understand Mom and me. Why, we haven't consciously challenged you to do any such a thing."

He sighed a little. Then, ignoring her denial, "I guess you've forgotten that our original plan for the establishment of this school provided for a lot of hard, honest work—by me and you. It was not to be deliberately handed to us on a silver platter by some individual philanthropist. No," he shook his head, "instead, we were to get married then start it on the proverbial shoestring. Remember?"

Ellen tried to hide her hurt amazement behind a smile which failed to register.

"Nonsense!" she said. "Surely you don't understand, Dewalt. As a matter of fact, I think you're being a little selfish. Evidently, you're considering no one but you and me in the matter. But we must first think of those we would help. Why should we hesitate to accept a sincere gift for our school when Negro youth are so much in need of it? It might take years and years, by the old shoe-string method, to come to their rescue. By accepting Mom's gift, we will be able actually to begin helping them within only a few months." She shook her head slowly and thoughtfully. "Really, Dewalt," she went on, "we must forget ourselves—our pride—and think of those who stand in need of our help. We must not forget that the very future of the race depends upon them."

For a minute, he was silent, as if he had not heard her. Then, she felt the end of the lounge on which he sat opposite her, expand as he lifted his weight from it. He clasped his hands behind him and strode, is if in deep thought, to the tall window which looked out upon the terrace that lay quietly beneath a starry sky.

Presently, she arose and followed him and stood silent beside him at the window. She felt that a yawning chasm separated them and was alarmed at the deep yearning in her heart to feel his hardened arms about her, drawing her close to him. Uneasily, almost frantically, she wondered if he yet loved her, or if these years of their separation and his hardship had divorced him from her.

Suddenly, he shifted his eyes from the stars outside and looked wistfully down upon her:

"And you mean to say that we're not to think of our personal happiness to the extent of getting married as we'd planned?" he said thickly.

Her heart lightened at the thought that perhaps he still cared for her.

"No," she denied, "I don't mean to say that exactly. It's just that —— well, perhaps you still don't understand ——"

"Now, don't hedge," he cautioned her accusingly. "I understand perfectly, and of course I have no right to blame you. You know," he continued after a sigh, "riches have a way of emancipating one from old interests. I suppose I've been a fool to expect to find you waiting to marry me. You certainly hinted nothing of the sort in your letter."

This from him brought a lump to her throat.

"Dewalt, please!" she cried softly. "Why, during these years, that's all I've done — — waited for you! You've still got me waiting, and every second of it grows more unbearable!"

Suddenly, she felt him grasp her, a little savagely, then draw her close to him—so close that she could feel the pounding of his heart.

"Darling!" he cried with deep emotion, "first of all, we're getting married — — right away!"

CHAPTER THIRTY

From that tense moment on, life assumed a new meaning for Ellen. To her, it became a revolving and purposeful cycle of achievement. At some juncture along its rapid and breathtaking revolutions, she married Dewalt Brooks, with the loving benedictions of her mother and the tender admiration of Mae who had now emerged from Northern University, a promising and much admired debutante.

Ellen never stopped once to take cognizance of the months and the years, perhaps, that passed excitingly on. Beside themselves, she and Dewalt were interested only in the fact that, upon a beautifully terraced knoll of land, the first unit of the Anice Vance College (named for Mom) of Practical Negro Education was nearing completion, and next fall, its massive doors would open to several hundred graduate Negro students. The two of them looked foward, with much zest, to devoting the remainder of their lives to its development.

*　　*　　*

The late summer evening was cool and pleasant, and Ellen and Dewalt strolled out of the yard of their comfortable cottage, across a shady, graveled street, onto the freshly landscaped campus of the Anice Vance College—their pride and joy!

Before them, like a classic architectural painting, the great brick and marble building, which represented the first unit of the new institution, stood limned against the brilliant rays of the setting sun behind it. Workmen who had been engaged in applying the finishing touches to it, had left for the day, and it was quiet and serent. It reared its domed roof four stories high and massive marble columns, reaching to the second story above an ornately arched doorway, marked the main entrance from which a broad, paved walk stretched, ribbon-like, across the campus.

Within several weeks now, scores of ambitious Negro students would be crossing that welcoming threshhold, and contemplation of this filled the hearts of the young husband and wife with unbounded gladness as the two strolled up the pavement to the newly furnished suite of administrative offices on the second floor where the architect's drawings and blue prints awaited their regular daily inspection.

Along its way, the white strip of pavement coiled through stately trees that had emerged from the hands of tree surgeons, beautifully pruned; their limbs and branches raised heavenward as if in obeisance to a creator who had seen fit to ordain that their environ should become that of a great Negro institution of learning— one which would not be dependent upon philanthropy from outside the Negro race; thus, one which would be free to dispense an education especially designed for the problems confronting Negroes.

There would be no prejudiced white officials out of whom appropriations must be wheedled by way of various and sundry forms of "bootlicking"! There would be no "Simon Legrees" constantly brandishing a psychological whip over its purposeful and sincere faculty members! Negro youth would be taught the true meaning of manhood and womanhood; they would leave this in-

stitution burbling over with enthusiasm and initiative—
ready to grapple with, and solve, the vital problems of
their race!

Suddenly, as the two were half-way to the building,
Ellen gripped Dewalt's hand, bringing him to a halt beside her. She was seeing a moving mirage ahead of
them. He looked down at her, and the smiling expression on her face told him that she was gloriously happy—
happier than he had ever before seen her—and he felt
that he must enjoy the moment with her.

"What is it you see, darling?" he asked indulgently.

She sighed ecstatically, her eyes still riveted to something she was seeing in the direction of the great new
building and the flaming sun which was setting behind it.

"A mirage, I suppose!" she answered him breathlessly. "The building has multiplied itself," she went on,
rapturously, "and —— and before us is the great Negro
university of the future! Look, dear! Do you see it?"
Her grip tightened on his hand.

"No, darling," he said in a low tone, "Suppose you
describe it to me!"

"Oh, Dewalt, it's wonderful!" she cried softly, "almost too wonderful to describe! Maybe —— maybe
we're on the very threshhold of Paradise! There are
great buildings —— many of them! and young men
and women, all Negroes, going in and out of them! Look,
darling —— they're all smiling! They're happy! —"
she paused as suddenly all, save the new building, vanished before her very eyes, and, coming back to earth,
she looked up to him in breathless amazement.

He smiled down into her glowing eyes, ,adoringly.

"And now it's all vanished?" he asked, then before
she could reply, added, "come along, sweetheart. Remember, the lights are not yet turned on, and we must
see those prints before it is dark." He nodded toward the
second story of the building: "We must get along, for,
at this moment, there's a greater need ——" he broke off
shortly as a slight shudder coursed over her, then added,

"— — above, for us." This last at the realization of the basis of her shudder.

She raised her face to him again, and their smiling eyes met.

"Yes!" she sighed exultantly, then, hand in hand, they walked along the remaining length of the pavement, into the arched doorway of the building.

THE END